WET

MORE AQUA EROTICA

WET

MORE AQUA EROTICA

WET
MORE AQUA EROTICA

EDITED BY MARY ANNE MOHANRAJ
PHOTOGRAPHY BY HOWARD SCHATZ

A MELCHER MEDIA DURABOOK

Published in the UK by Dorling Kindersley Limited
80 Strand, London WC2R 0RL
www.dk.com
in association with

 MELCHER MEDIA

124 West 13th Street
New York, NY 10011
www.melcher.com

Publisher: Charles Melcher
Senior Editor: Duncan Bock
Associate Editor: Lia Ronnen
Production Director: Andrea Hirsh

Book Design by Elizabeth Van Itallie

Published in the USA by Three Rivers Press,
New York, New York, a division of Random House, Inc.
www.randomhouse.com

Durabook™, patent no. 6,773,034, is a trademark of Melcher Media, Inc. The Durabook™
format utilizes revolutionary technology and is completely waterproof and highly durable.

Printed in China

A CIP catalogue record for this book is available from the British Library.

ISBN-13: 978-1-59591-026-4
ISBN-10: 1-59591-026-3

First Edition

CONTENTS

INTRODUCTION
BY MARY ANNE MOHANRAJ

Why write erotica?

There are many answers, ranging from a desire to speak openly about that which has been hidden in our society, to a desire to push at a writer's own boundaries, to a sheer pleasure in the gorgeous sensuality of the images and language surrounding sexuality. Every writer will have her own reasons to write erotic fiction. What I personally find most valuable about erotica is the window it offers us into hidden character, into the vagaries of the human heart. If the job of fiction is to examine what it means to be human, I would argue that erotic fiction offers us a unique perspective on that examination.

People are different during sex—aspects of their private selves come forth that would never appear in public otherwise. It is in sex that we have an opportunity to become most naked—not just physically vulnerable but mentally and emotionally as well. We expose our fears, and worse, our desires, to another's view and, in so doing, risk their fear, their ridicule, their repulsion. Part of the power of sex lies in how very frightening it can be; when we walk out on that emotional tightrope, it can be a long way down.

Of course, we hope not to fall. We hope to balance well, or even to grow wings, to soar with a partner (or partners) to pleasurable heights that we could never reach alone. We hope that when we lay ourselves bare before another's gaze, that he/she will find us beautiful, desirable—that he/she will match us in this risky game and lay themselves open as well. That is the lure of intimacy, the promise of shared fears that may be overcome by desire—leading in the end to great pleasure. The rewards are potentially tremendous, but the risk is always there as well.

In this collection, many of these authors seem very much aware of the potential risks that underlie their trembling approaches to desire. I am struck by the poignant tone that accompanies many, if not most, of these tales. Many of the stories begin with pain, with a current of sorrow and fear that the characters must rise above in order to find pleasure and joy. And in some stories, the erotic energy of the tale seems inextricably wedded to pain—to sadness or fear that moves through the heart of the story and, in the end, makes it even more powerfully sexual.

In several tales, the characters are oddly separate; the lovers are drawn together, yet their own fears work to keep them apart. In Bill Noble's "Salt," a tropical storm and the threat of death is required to finally bring two frightened loners together; in Jeffrey Chapman's "On the Uses of a Bathtub," it is exhaustion and a cold, penetrating winter that at first separates a couple. In Mary Gaitskill's "The Ugly Cock Dance," the passage of years and each partner's difficulty in believing in his or her own continued desirability keep a husband and wife apart. And in Diane Kepler's "Sakura," it is a difference in age between a young Japanese girl and an American graduate student that bars their path to pleasure. In each of these stories, the characters transcend their difficulties to find desire, followed by intense sexual pleasure—but it is never an easy passage.

The trend continues with other stories in the collection, and in some of them, pain continues even through the pleasure, as in Dave Smeds's "Depths," the tale of a man having an affair with a married woman, an affair he must consummate in stolen moments. In Chris Jones's "Shelter from the Storm," a S/M scene brings sexual release but denies the intimacy the protagonist desires. In J. Hartman's story, "The Flood," a threesome finds joy, and even healing—but their tenure together is fleeting; the fragile bond they create cannot survive in the America of the 1930s. Loren MacLeod's "Giselle" gives us pleasure only in our heroine's past; her present is bleak and frightening, and her future uncertain. And in Simon Sheppard's "Number Fourteen," while the protagonist finds brief and intense access to the sexual fantasies of his childhood comic books, in the end, he must return to the adult world, with its very different sexual patterns. I think you will find the pain in these stories doesn't detract from the pleasure—rather, it adds to it, heightens the pitch of emotion to bring characters and readers to shattering climaxes.

Of course, there are a few light tales in this book—even the most intense lover needs a rest now and then. Jack Murnighan's "Slick" and Cecilia Tan's "Rite of Spring" are delightful romps, each in their own way. Nisi Shawl's "Vapors" is a charming tale of a young girl's adventures in self-pleasuring, and Connie Wilkins's "Seafood Cocktail" takes us into the strangely twisted world of reality TV, the way it ought to be done.

But for most of the stories in this collection, the sexual heat of the tales comes from the varied ways in which the characters put themselves at risk. The emotional tides that run through these stories are often difficult for their characters to navigate; it might be easier to walk away from the storm of desire and remain on the dry shore.

But honest desire is rarely safe, and even in the lightest story, pleasure always carries with it the possibility of pain. In the end, it seems that this danger provides, for some at least, an access to a far greater pleasure than what they might have otherwise found, a pleasure that is intense enough to lure us onward, seeking ever-greater heights. . . .

SALT

BY BILL NOBLE

The week Shoshanna left her, snow dusted the *pali* for the first time in memory. It was so cold she could hear the year's crop of mangoes plopping green off the trees. Then, with the white still clinging to the cliffs, rangers came and burned her shack down. And nearly busted her, too, if she hadn't run. That was a big deal—and it was a big deal, too, when some hippie in a homemade pigskin vest walked up and found her cold and crying by the ashes.

Mandy wiped her face on the back of a sooty hand and glared, but the hippie wrapped his jacket around her shoulders till she stopped shivering. He didn't seem to need to talk much, and sure as shit she had no need to talk to him, so they just stood, surrounded by guava and tangled lantana, listening to the embers pop.

"Nothin' to salvage," he said after a while. And then, looking her nakedness up and down, "Warm enough?"

Part of her wanted to say *Fuck you,* what with the man smell and the pigskin stink, but she managed to keep her mouth shut.

"Got some food in my boat." Her belly cramped at the word *food,* so she turned and looked at him for the first time.

He had a gray ponytail, a lean belly, and a pair of raggedy shorts that must have been white once. No underwear: Mandy could glimpse the crookedy dangle of a testicle.

Salt. That's the other smell. He's a paddler. She pulled the jacket tighter and grunted, "I guess I could eat." She fought some brief internal battle and then looked at him again. "Thanks."

"Hike back to the beach?" And then he seemed afraid he'd overstepped. "Or I could bring stuff up."

"Nah," she said, and turned toward the narrow canebrake trail that led down Kalalau Valley toward the ocean. "You saw the fire?" she asked, half-surprised she was talking to him. She shook her tangled hair out and tied it back, shimmying her bare butt as she went down the trail. *Why the hell am I doing that?* And then her grief over Shoshanna slammed back.

"Saw the smoke, and I'd heard about the rangers roustin' people, all up and down the Na Pali Coast. Tryin' t'make the world safe for tourists," he said. "How long were you livin' here?"

She stopped and handed him back his jacket. "What's your name?" she asked.

"Pranha," he said. "Wanna little bud?" He grubbed a small brass cylinder and wrinkled rolling papers out of his shorts.

"I'm Mandy. No, I don't smoke. Don't wear clothes much, either," she said, gesturing at the jacket. "But . . . I appreciate the help." The words tumbled out. She hadn't had much occasion to talk this last week.

They sat cross-legged when they reached the beach and ate Ry-Krisp and pineapple under the steady roar of the surf. The guy never sneaked a look at her snatch, not once. It was making her wet, wanting him to. *Gay?* She shrugged. *Ah, who gives a shit?*

The sun was already flattening on the horizon. "So, how long you been livin' in Kalalau?"

"Six years in Kaua'i, four years out here."

He tore open another packet of crackers and sized her up. Mandy was about as brown as a haole could get, long, tight-curled hair, jujube nipples, bodacious hips. Hippies like her lived all over the islands, in the remotest places. "From LA?"

She bristled. *What the fuck is it to you?* But she gave it up and said, "San Bernardino. Sonofabitch husband, fucked-up job, too much dope and loud music. You?"

"Anaheim," he said, and they both snorted.

"My partner left," she said, pissed she'd said it as soon as the words were out.

"Where'd he go?"

"She," she said, testing. The guy didn't flinch. And even letting him know she was a lesbian didn't get him to look at her snatch.

He squinted. "What you plannin' on doing?"

Tears came. She jumped up and stalked away down the beach. When she came back at dusk, he had a tarp spread in the lee of some pandanus. He looked up. "I just roll up in it at night," he said. "Even tonight, that'll be warm enough. Join me if you want, no hassles."

She stomped off again but returned before full dark. A shama thrush was weaving its fluted music with the slow beat of the surf.

"No sex," she said, looking as ferocious as she could with a blurry, tear-stained face.

"No sex," he agreed. It was funny—the guy had hardly any male vibes. He raised the edge of the tarp to invite her in; his nakedness startled her for a moment, then she lay down, naked herself, and he folded the tarp over them. She flung an arm over his chest, challenging him with her eyes. It was good to hold a body, even if it wasn't Shoshanna's. Even if it was a man's.

Mandy woke curled tight around Pranha. He was deep in sleep, mouth open, breath rattling in his throat. He had an erection. She fingered its length, amused at the heat of it, moved by the slow pulse along its underside. Men. Horny even when they're asleep, for Chrissakes. And then she remembered Shoshanna again, the way she'd taken her by the shoulders that very first night—her first woman—and kissed her till they almost fell over. She remembered the sureness and force as her hand went between Shoshanna's legs, and the sounds she brought out of her . . . and Mandy, lying with a strange man, felt the familiar knife of her wanting.

Salt tears spilled over Pranha's sleeping shoulder. She gripped his cock until his arousal faded, and, after, kept him cupped tiny in her hand until sleep reclaimed her.

In the morning Pranha said he was splitting. "You can come," he said. He gestured at his weathered kayak with its homemade outrigger and tattered sail wound around a jerry-rigged mast.

"Where're you headed?"

"Around to Hanapepe."

"I hate that side of the island, Hanapepe and Lihue and all the fucking tourists. I've got friends in Hanalei. I might go there, I guess, if you were going."

"Well . . ." Pranha looked doubtful. "The trades are pretty fresh. Be rough headin' that way. Big seas."

Mandy looked at the kayak, its red deck bleached mottled pink from the sun. Bags of gear were stuffed around the seats in the two narrow cockpits. A scratched marijuana-leaf decal fanned over the bow; a tattered rainbow flag hung on the mast. In that moment, she was overwhelmed by the need to leave Kalalau, to get away from the smell of guava, the memories of Shoshanna, the ashes of her home. The ocean had a sharp tang, urgent, like freedom, and the wind teased her breasts. "If you'll go to Hanalei, I'll go with you. I don't care about the waves."

He reached for his salt-stiffened shorts and pulled them on self-consciously while she eyed the ungainly flapping of his cock. "We could try," he said.

She stood up, showing him her muscled belly, her smooth, solid biceps. "I'm strong," she said. "I can paddle. I'll help you drag the boat down." For the first time, she caught him looking at her breasts.

Pranha looked up to the *pali,* where the snow was only a faint filigree now. He looked to sea. Big rollers far out, their white backs churning in and out of view. He sat facing the breakers, chin on his knees. He rolled a joint, lit it, and sucked it deeply. After a while he turned and looked at the broad-hipped, naked woman, tear tracks and ash still dark on her cheeks. He took another long toke, studying the sea. "Okay," he said, letting the smoke out. He stashed the joint and stood.

As they dragged the boat to the surf line, Mandy challenged him. "How come you don't want sex with me?"

"You asked me not to."

"Bullshit."

He tested the lashings on the mast. "Anyway, it's not about you."

"Broken heart?" she said, a twist of recognition in her gut.

Pranha's callused, cracked fingers stroked the kayak's flank, not looking at her. He unclipped the spare paddle and offered it to her. "Too much of a hassle. All that shit. You can really paddle?"

Sometimes missing Shoshanna was like a knife. "Suppose I asked you to lick me. Would you?"

He was watching the ocean. "Look," he said, "we've got an easy set comin' in," and shoved the kayak bowfirst into the surge.

They smashed through three big breakers and found themselves at sea. Mandy was breathless with the effort. The water was a fierce dark blue, and the wind, a scant hundred yards offshore, was fiercer. She craned back to look at him, licking the salt from her lips. "I didn't know it'd be blowing so hard. Is this okay?"

"Paddle. We gotta stay in close, under the *pali*. Farther out it's really blowing. Up at Ke'e there'll be fifteen-foot swells. Mandy?"

Over her shoulder, she raised an eyebrow at him.

"If you wanted, I'd lick you." He looked her calmly in the eye when he said it, then looked away, over the water.

A knot of desire tied itself behind her pelvic arch, and then twisted tighter in refusal. Her old contempt for her husband bubbled up. "What're you, an angel of mercy?" He was leaning hard into each stroke. He didn't look up.

"Or you've got herpes." Acid in her saliva bunched her jaw muscles. *I'll make this son of a bitch respond!*

His pale blue eyes came up to catch hers. "You lived alone much before this?"

It was hard to paddle and keep looking back at him. As the water dried on her bare flesh, the sun began to warm her. She softened her voice. "You had a hard-on last night. I touched a man for the first time in . . . I don't know. Ten years. I kind of hate men. I held you for a couple of hours, I guess, and it made me horny." Sometimes thinking about Shoshanna, about stumbling on her in the little bakery in Kilauea, about kissing her woman's softness, made her feel the knife actually ripping her gut. She raised her gray eyes to Pranha.

"Shit," he said, his eyes wide.

It took her a long minute to realize he wasn't talking to her. She turned, and a dark wall of water was rushing at her. It tore the paddle from her hands and buried her. Deep. The sea forced its way into her stomach, bitter and flat. In the roar of the water, something in the boat groaned, a long, wrenching groan, and the sea spun her over and over, trapped in the cockpit.

Somehow she squirmed free and, after kicking toward the light for far too long a time, broke the surface. She spat salt, cursing and coughing. The kayak wallowed belly-up. One outrigger had snapped; the other had wrenched loose from the pontoon, which was now attached to the boat by only two fragile lines. The mast with its furled sail tipped over a downwind swell and vanished. "Hey!" she yelled, and then she remembered his name. "Pran-HA! Heyyyy!"

"I'm here," he said, and she discovered him clinging to the stern a few feet behind her.

"What the hell! What do we do?" She was still coughing up water.

"Boost the stern and drain her. Then the bow. If we're lucky, we get enough water out to right her." His calmness pissed her off.

"Are we okay?"

"Dunno."

"What the fuck does that mean?"

"Well, we've got one paddle and we can rerig the pontoon. Maybe by the time we get paddlin' again we won't be too far off-shore to get back."

"Get back to fucking where?!"

"That's Kaua'i," he said, gesturing into the driving wind. He waved downwind. "And that's the Marianas. Thousand miles. We probably don't wanna go that way."

They paddled until dark, passing the paddle back and forth as they tired. Pranha guessed they were three miles out, losing the battle to regain Kaua'i. He shrugged and took inventory: three boxes of crackers, a hand of bananas, and a scant gallon of water.

The trades blew all night, and they paddled into them. The good news, at dawn, was that they weren't any farther offshore. The bad news was that they were exhausted. Their hands were blistered and brine-soaked, bleeding.

Mandy squirmed around and knelt in her seat facing Pranha. *What's it take to get through to this hippy hermit?* "We're not going to have sex, are we?"

"Still thinkin' about sex out here? You're not doing so bad." His tired face creased into a smile.

"I don't want to die alone, I guess."

He paddled in silence for several minutes, then braced the paddle and guided them over a roller. He reached from the stern cockpit until they could clasp their swollen, raw hands. "Me neither. I just didn't know that till a coupla minutes ago."

It wasn't easy to talk, but in bits and pieces they told each other about themselves. Mandy shared her grief over Shoshanna, her anger about men and shit jobs and LA. She told about her four years of love, and yoga, and the crazy, intense woman-sex that just made her hungrier, about no clothes and all the guavas anybody could ever eat. Pranha watched her luminous eyes, her mobile, too-large mouth, as she twisted half toward him in the bow cockpit. When she was through, he talked about his world. "I said sex was too much hassle," he said. "But everything's a hassle. Look," he said after a pause, "if we get outta this . . ."

"If we get to shore," Mandy grinned, "I'm gonna jump your bones. I'm gonna fuck you till you holler. I'm gonna make you hump me like a cocker spaniel. I'm gonna suck your weenie half off just to prove I'm not prejudiced and then I'm gonna stuff your head in my snatch for at least three hours. And then I'm gonna kick your ass. Shut up and pass the paddle. You look like shit."

As he leaned forward, she glimpsed a full erection pushing from the fringe of his shorts. Cock, mouth, fingers: it didn't matter how she got it done. She wanted a beating heart laid against hers. She closed her eyes and let arousal take her, let it invade her exhaustion, grateful to be thrumming like this even in the middle of the fucking goddamn ocean.

The shark came at midday, a fin thirty feet out, circling, then sliding under the waves.

"What'll we do?" Mandy's diaphragm wouldn't let her breathe.

"I dunno. It's a mako, I think. If it bumps us, try t'hit it in the nose with the paddle or your fist. They say that makes 'em go away."

"Hit a shark with my fist?!"

Pranha raised a tired arm. "Either that, or it breaks up the boat, maybe, and eats us."

After a few hours it disappeared, and exhaustion hit full force. Mandy slumped in the forward cockpit and went unconscious. She woke later, confused, guilty that she hadn't been paddling. Head on the deck, she stared blankly at the water, only gradually realizing that she was looking into a single small, unblinking eye, inches below the surface. She jolted upright.

"Go easy." It was Pranha, behind her. "It's just hanging out in the shade of the boat. Don't do anything weird."

The shark, an arm's length away, was nearly as long as the kayak. "Hey," she said to Pranha in a small voice, "I'm not thinking about sex anymore." But she was. *Sand under my back. Pranha on top of me, fucking me. No— Shoshanna, and I'm on top. She calls my name. I dig my fingers into the earth to hold us safe.* The shark's unmoving eye made her want to touch herself. To come. To do any fucking thing but be there skewered by that cold gaze.

That second night, under the stars, they could no longer see the shark, and that was worse. Thirst clogged their throats, made it hard to talk.

The wind had slacked off with nightfall. By the time the Southern Cross inched over the horizon, the sea was nearly windless. Past pain, they paddled until their arms would no longer lift from the deck, then traded off. By midnight the island had risen, cutting off more of the northeastern sky. The paddle bit into the phosphorescent water, stroke after stroke. After long hours, the Cross sank behind them and first light grew ahead. The swells lifted, glassy smooth. The *pali* showed detail now: the slash of canyons, pale cliffs, forest.

Three tropic birds flew low over their bow. Mandy wanted to call to them, lovely in the pearly light, but she couldn't speak. Pranha nudged the paddle against her back. She took it and began to stroke.

"Mandy."

She could only paddle, voiceless.

"Mandy. We're gonna make it. Follow the shore. We can put in at Ke'e. Go in close while we can: the wind's gonna come back."

When sun touched the water around them, they were just outside the breakers, under the unbroken rise of the *pali*. They could hear birdsong ashore. The shark circled once, soundless, then sank into the depths. Salt rasped and itched in every fold of their skin.

It took another hour to reach the reef off Ke'e. Pranha found the entrance and they rode a last big swell into the lagoon. The water swirled turquoise under them, darting with fish. *About fucking time,* she thought, tears welling up again. When they beached, their legs wouldn't support them; clutching each other, they fell onto the sand.

The first tourists appeared at midmorning. Pranha sat up. His eyes and lips were salt-rimed, white against his sunburnt skin. "Now who looks like shit?" he said, and she wanted to laugh at him—with him—but her belly muscles were too tired to force out a sound. "C'mon," he said, "I know a place we can sleep."

They staggered together past the cinder-block restrooms, stopping to fill Pranha's jug with water. By the trash cans, some picnicker had dumped a six-pack of soda. Pranha grappled it into the crook of an arm. He led her to a small, fern-fringed clearing. They drank all six sodas and most of the water, then crumpled into each other's arms.

When Mandy woke, late sun was slanting through the leaves of a breadfruit tree, and Pranha was still in her arms. She wanted to caress him, as much for herself as for any pleasure he might find in it, but her hands were unusable, paddles at the ends of leaden arms, stiff with blood and salt.

She looked at Pranha, sun-scalded and raw, sunk in sleep that seemed close to the edge of coma. Naked herself, she ran her eyes over the male body, clothed only in its disreputable shorts. Awkwardly, she pried the button loose on the shorts and tugged them off him.

Jesus. What am I doing? Every muscle ached. Her long dark hair was stiff and filthy. Two days of sunburn had seared her face, made the breeze unbearable on her tender breasts. *My hands are a mess!* It'd be days before she could use them. But she hungered to touch this man. She wanted his cock. The need to anchor herself in another body was stronger than any anger she still held, stronger than any particular missing.

She bent over him. She licked, and recoiled at the bitter sea grit dissolving on her tongue. She licked again, and found it easier. And again, until she could pull him into her mouth.

He was small and unaroused—beyond arousal, maybe—but it didn't matter. She tongued the convolutions of his cockhead, round and round, finding a rhythm for sore muscles and stiff face. She knelt clumsily, her useless hands palms-up on her knees, bowed over him. She lost herself in sucking.

She began to tug, stretching him out rubbery and thin, searching out the cords and vessels with her tongue. She let her breath spill into his nest of hair and inhaled the smell that came back from him.

With the back of a hand she stroked his chest and lean belly. This brought his first response: he swelled in her mouth and at last became hard. She looked up. He was watching. She bobbed on him, grinning with her eyes. It was evening, and birds were singing again. *Whoo-eee! I'm going to do you, boy!*

He braced an arm under his head, observing. Over a long aimless time as she sucked, he softened, then swelled again. She ran her tongue tip down the bitter-salt midline of his scrotum and it tightened. She sucked harder on his cock, and his hips followed her. His mouth gaped.

After a while his arms canted out as if he were being crucified. His head arched back and the taste of him changed in her mouth. The long muscles in his legs took up a heavy shaking. His body lifted, bridged between his heels and the back of his neck. He hung like that as she devoured him, bent above him as if in prayer. *Follow me, boy. Fly!*

"Wait," he rasped, his voice salt-scalded. "Wait."

"What? What's wrong?" Mandy pulled away.

His voice failed and he could only mouth the words: "Let . . . me."

He twisted and thrust his face into her sex. She flooded with moisture, her own scent coiling up to her nostrils: brine and musk and exhaustion. His tongue searched her, his blue eyes holding hers from the thicket of her black bush. The furry insistence of his beard made the cords in her thighs ache.

She jammed his shorts under his head for a pillow and fell against his mouth, whispering wordlessly. Braced on her knuckles, oblivious to the pain in her hands and shoulders, she humped. His face rolled and twisted under her, his eyes shut tight now, worshipping. She locked her thighs against his ribs.

Yeah. Her back straightened. She couldn't contain her climax. It ballooned until it was bigger, somehow, than her body, stretching her bones, filling her mouth with a wavering music. *Please!* She rode so high on his face *please fucking please* she was afraid she'd suffocate him *please* but nothing could stop her now, nothing. *Yeah! Yeah!*

Coming was like drowning. *No, like being pitched into the fucking sun. Like burning down around myself.* Something far back in her called *Shoshanna!* and she fell face-first to the ground.

Long after, she searched out Pranha's face. His pale eyes waited, solemn. She saw loops of semen strung over his chest, already thinning and beginning to run. *A man,* she thought. It didn't matter. She opened her mouth over his. His hand clamped the back of her neck and crushed her closer.

As the swift tropical night flooded through the palm grove, he hobbled to the boat and brought his tarp. They slept.

The third morning he searched out a long-tailed shirt from among his gear, decency enough, they thought, for her to face civilization. The cloth clung alien and imprisoning, harsh from the sea. They hid the kayak in the ferns, limped to the road, and hung out their thumbs. *Shit,* she thought, *I'm back.*

A rattling island car picked them up. After they disappeared toward Hanalei, the narrow road lay empty for a long time. Breakers boomed on the reef. Small waves lapped the coral sand and sighed back into the wide salt of the sea. ◆

SAKURA

BY DIANE KEPLER

ICHI

It is that magical week when the cherry blossoms are just past the height of their fullness and their petals begin to flutter down in a fragrant, pink rain. The streets and avenues are quieter some-how, and more comfortable, as if wrapped in a rosy quilt.

The pastel-patterned sidewalk occupies Hiroe as she makes her way home from school. Her gait is dreamlike. At times she slows, lingering under the perfumed boughs, lifting up her face to feel the petals alight. They dot her cheeks and the fragile domes of her closed eyes. Each contact is like a kiss. She smiles to herself, imagining the real kisses that are soon to follow.

He waits for her at the temple. Not grand Kinkakuji or ancient Daitokoji, where the other foreigners swarm like so many pale moths, but the humble sanctuary that marks the spot where her lane joins the main thoroughfare. He is burning incense when she arrives. As always, she is reminded of the first time she saw him there, kneeling composedly, and, as far as she knew from her casual acquaintance with Jodo Buddhism, doing everything exactly right.

NI

She waited, on that first day, until he'd finished his devotions. Waited and then hurried forward as he was stepping into his shoes back on the wide, wooden verandah of the shrine.

"Ex-cu-suh me, pu-ree-suh," she managed after a great deal of shifting from foot to foot. For the first time, Hiroe had cause to regret all those notes she kept passing during English class. But he was so beautiful. She had to say something.

When he turned she saw how wide his eyes were and, when he answered in polite, idiomatic Japanese, how elegant his smile.

"I'm sorry, Miss, could you repeat that? I didn't understand."

"A Kyoto accent," she'd whispered to Rei and Asuka at school the next day. "It's as if he'd lived here all his life."

"Is he handsome?" Asuka urged.

Hiroe lifted her chin. "Remember Yuji from the WeissKreuz anime?"

Rei gaped at her. "You mean the tall blonde?"

"Exactly. And not only that, he's smart! He's studying history at Kyodai—politics and culture of the Muromachi era. Aunt Setsuko said he knows as many kanji as she does. He's practically a poet."

"How does your aunt know him?"

"That's the very best part," Hiroe sighed. "He's staying at her guesthouse!"

"Right down the street from you," breathed Rei.

"Fifty-four steps," confirmed Hiroe with a nod of her head. "I counted."

Rei and Asuka drew their friend into an exuberant, three-way hug. "Iyaaa!" they shrieked in unison. "You're so lucky!"

"So, does he like you?" Rei prompted, which forced an awkward pause. Hiroe dropped her eyes, scuffing one shoe along the paving stones of the schoolyard. "I don't know. At first I thought no, but then ... How can I tell?"

"That's easy," said Asuka. "He buys you things."

SAN

"Happy birthday," John murmured as the subway gathered speed. It was a Thursday afternoon, an occasion that had shot up Hiroe's "Favorite Times of the Week" chart ever since she'd met him by chance on his way home from classes and found that their schedules coincided. She'd lain in wait for him ever since.

From his knapsack he conjured a small, flat package, elegantly wrapped in the old style in a square of plum-coloured silk. It was a favorite trick of Aunt Setsuko's, and Hiroe couldn't help wondering if her aunt had taught him or if he'd figured it out himself.

She gave a small cry of happiness and then worked at the knot, concealing neither her eagerness nor her disenchantment when her long-awaited present turned out to be just a book of classical poems, and a used one at that.

How ... boring, she thought. And how cheap! This was nothing like the extravagant presents from the salarymen who wooed some of her classmates.

John watched her closely and then gave a little grin. "I know, it's not what you expected. But I'm hoping you'll appreciate it someday."

"No I won't," Hiroe pouted, squinting at the elegant type. "Who cares about standing under a straw roof in the rain?" Yet despite her moue of displeasure, she was more happy than not. Finally, after months of waiting, summer slipping into autumn, he had given her a gift. And now, a lucky break. A rude little dumpling of a boy who seemed destined for the sumo ring had wedged himself in on her other side, giving Hiroe the excuse to press up against John, hip to hip and thigh to thigh, so that, whenever the subway slowed, she could lean in to him, pretending it was her own inertia that took her.

The doors closed, the train gathered speed. Hiroe dared a glance at the object of her affection.

"Now a book of love poems," she murmured, with her toes touching prettily and her eyes as round as she could make them, "that would be an ideal gift for a girl like me. Why don't you give me a book of love poems, John?"

He scratched his head, pretending to think. "Uh, because we're not lovers?"

"Yes we are. I love you, and you're just crazy about me!"

That brought an honest laugh out of him. "Ah, Hiroe, Hiroe," he murmured, shaking his head.

She thrilled at the way he said her name: gently, with each of the three syllables glowing as if lit up from the inside.

"We should take a honeymoon," she declared. It was half a joke, but as always, it was also half serious.

John raised an eyebrow at her. "You're getting ambitious. First you suggested a tryst in the park, then a love hotel, and now an honest-to-goodness trip somewhere? Hm . . ." he pretended to consider, "I hear Singapore's popular. My savings could probably get us to Osaka."

"I have money. I can pay."

He pursed his lips and then twisted them in an expression she couldn't understand. "You probably could at that. Tell you what. Give me a while to pick out a destination."

"How long?"

His sweeping glance was appraising but not unkind. "How about a few years?"

Hiroe went red and looked down at her lap. The book of poems was still there, also red against the blue pleated skirt of her school uniform.

"Maybe in your backwards country they have some crazy laws, but—"

He sighed and leaned back against the subway seat, fitting the heels of his palms against his closed eyes. "It's got nothing to do with laws, Hiroe. It's about consent, and the ability to know what you're agreeing to—we've been through this before. And I wish you'd stop asking all the time." He took down his hands and gave her a meaningful look. "Do you have *any* idea what that's like for me?"

"No," she sulked, and this time her expression was real.

John turned toward her then. He put an arm around her shoulders. "Have you ever heard of the Chinese water torture?"

Hiroe was shocked and amazed. He had his *arm* around her! In public, no less—like they were a real couple. She fought to keep her breathing even. Betraying her excitement might dislodge him.

"Most likely some product of another barbarian culture," she said loftily.

"Ah, the youth of today," he sighed and ran a finger along

Hiroe's forehead, stroking the roots of her glossy black hair. "Please, allow me to educate you. "

"What does this have to do with—"

"Shh," he whispered. "Now lie back."

Hiroe felt a gentle tap on her forehead. She knew it was his finger, but it felt as if a drop of water had landed there. She felt another tap after a few seconds, and then another. Hiroe's head rolled in time to the swaying of the subway car, but somehow he always managed to touch the exact same spot.

"John—"

His opposing hand on her shoulder held her in place. The tapping continued, becoming very annoying very quickly.

"Quit it!" Hiroe twisted away.

He smiled at her. "Terrible, isn't it? The Chinese used to interrogate prisoners this way. They'd tie people down, suspend a water clock over them, and let the droplets fall, just like that, for hours or days. Sometimes people went insane."

He leaned in close and his voice was barely a whisper. "That's what it's like for me when you keep asking all the time."

SHI

Hiroe, entranced by the blossoms, has taken longer than usual on her walk home from school. Yet he is there, at the temple.

He is kneeling with his back to her, as still as a lake in winter. She doesn't dare interrupt his meditation—at least not at first. But after a time, worry steals in. Is he angry that she is late? Did he even hear her approach? It wouldn't do to call his name, but . . .

Carefully, she slips off her shoes and kneels down beside him.

"Why are you here burning incense all the time?" she whispers in the semidarkness.

"Usually it's to ask Amida Buddha for guidance." His measured words rise like smoke toward the wooden rafters. His gaze is also directed upward, until he directs it to her dark and shining eyes. "But sometimes I also ask for forgiveness."

She shivers.

On the tatami mat in front of him, Hiroe sees a bag from Kyobuy, the new department store near the university.

"What's in there?"

"You're a curious little girl, aren't you?"

"Is it a present for me?"

"Perhaps. Or it might be for me. One never can tell."

He rises fluidly, makes a final obeisance to the Buddha image, and then strides to the porch to find his shoes.

"Where are we going?" chirps Hiroe, stuffing her feet into her black tie-ups, usually fashionable but now a nuisance. She lets the laces dangle, clattering down the steps after him.

He strides quickly through the mosaic of fallen cherry blossoms, snow white in the light of the streetlamps. His pace is brisk. She has to run to catch up.

"Where are we *going*?"

"You'll see."

It is in fact a teahouse in the heart of Gion, one that used to host geisha in bygone days. Hiroe is aghast at being taken to such an elegant place in her school uniform, while he's almost unbearably handsome in his khakis and a white button-down. But when she tells him as much, he laughs.

"So I was supposed to have let you go home to change? I'm sure your mother would have just let you breeze on out again."

Hiroe hadn't thought of that.

"Where do your parents think you are, anyway?"

"At Rei's house. Studying."

"Ah, of course." His expression is unreadable and dark somehow. For the first time, Hiroe feels a bit apprehensive.

The hostess seats them in a private room, with a black lacquered table in the center. There is a view of the courtyard—some greenery and a pond. A heartbeat after the hostess leaves, the paper screen slides back to admit a cheerful woman with a tea service. There are cups on the tray, a pot of steaming water, and a small porcelain bowl with tea itself. As she leaves, John tips her. The yen notes are discreetly folded, but Hiroe realizes this is much more than the average gratuity.

Once their server has padded noiselessly away, John turns to her.

"Well, my dear, we're alone now."

She sits still, wondering what he'll do next.

"Don't you want to kiss me?"

She blinks. It takes a moment for her to realize that he really expects it of her, that he won't move until she acts first. Afraid and yet mesmerized by the beautiful shape of his lips, she slides off of her cushion and crawls to where he sits quite composedly. Her first kiss is delicate—just a brush of his cheek with lips sweetly pursed—yet while he doesn't flinch away, he doesn't kiss her back either.

She draws nearer. She takes his face in her hands. With a thumb on each cheekbone she traces them, traces the contours of his eyes and then closes them. His nose and chin are the targets of her kisses, and then his mouth. When their lips touch he returns the kiss at last. The caress of his mouth is indeed as she imagined: as soft as the petals falling silently in the streets outside, but warmer. There is a perfume to him, too—a wonderful manly scent that she'd never noticed because she'd never come this close. His breath wafts across her nose and her lashes, causing a shiver to course through her, and a stirring, farther down.

His kisses are chaste, gentle. After a time Hiroe tries to speed them into something more passionate, but each time he draws away. She is kneeling to one side of him. He has not moved except to turn his head. The effort of rising to meet his lips is telling. Her thighs quiver with the strain of it. It makes her aware of the growing heat between them.

"Hiroe, permit me something."

She leans against him, the top of her head against the center of his chest, but she is looking at the tatami mats to one side and not into his lap because she's shy about what has grown there.

"Anything."

She can feel his smile. "Just what I wanted to hear."

He pushes her back and dips a careful finger into the water for the tea, which is still steaming. Fleetingly, he frowns.

"I want you to sit up here on the table facing me."

Hiroe opens her eyes. He is putting the tray with the tea things on the floor, making room.

"Sit? On the table?" It's a preposterous suggestion, as if he'd asked her to eat dinner off a chair.

"Shh. I'm going to give you your present now."

GO

Hiroe shuffled glumly out into the schoolyard. On either side of her, Rei and Asuka chattered merrily, but she couldn't find it in her to join them. The chill winter air nipped at her knees and nose, reminding her that despite these weeks upon weeks of carefully spaced intervals of flirting with John and ignoring him, nothing had changed.

"Keep after him," Asuka advised when Hiroe appealed to them for help.

"You must be like the river," said Rei, who was hopelessly addicted to historical dramas and fond of wise-woman sayings. "The water is soft, but patient. In time, it wears down even the hardest stone."

"Even the *hardest* stone," echoed Asuka, with a grin.

But despite all of Hiroe's efforts, John didn't give in—not when she flirted and not when she cried and not even when she called him one desperate night after her bath.

"John, I need you." Hiroe gripped the receiver with one hand, her other wandering. If she closed her eyes she could imagine him standing there at the common phone in the hallway at Aunt Setsuko's.

"Aren't you worried about your parents hearing you talking this way?"

"Mother's having her bath, and Father's out drinking with his colleagues. I am free to talk to my boyfriend however I please."

A sigh from the other end. "I see. Well, you'd better hang up then, he might be trying to call you."

"You silly . . ." She giggled, tracing the downy lips of her sex through a clean pair of cotton panties.

"Hiroe, I have to go. I have lots of work tonight."

"I can help," she offered, desperate now.

"I doubt it. My assignment is to write a poem in the style of Fujiwara no Sadai."

"I could write if for you! On your stomach, with a brush and ink. Our lovemaking would inspire me."

He laughed out loud. "Yes, I could just see myself untucking my shirt in front of the class tomorrow. I can hear my thesis advisor now: 'Whose is this terrible calligraphy?'"

He'd meant it to be funny, but she hung up the phone in a rage.

RYOKU

Her heart was sore with the agony of yet another refusal. Still, it did not stop Hiroe from drifting past the guest house on her way to school. But when she saw him looking mussed, and as if he'd only just stepped into his shoes, Hiroe hurried past.

"Good morning," he said with exaggerated politeness. His eyes looked small in the morning light and his shirt was wrinkled.

"Leave me alone," she shot back.

"Well, that's quite a change from last night."

"I'm a changed woman," she said airily, "one who'll forget you by taking another lover."

"Taking a lover, you mean."

She quickened her pace. "There are a lots of boys at school who would kill or die to have me." This was not precisely true, but with a bit of advertising, she could probably make it so.

"Hiroe." He stopped walking, and after a few steps she did, too. "I told you to forget this."

"I am."

"No, I mean really forget it." He sighed. "I'm tired of this."

"Tired of what?"

"Of you trying to force everything to be the way you want it. I told you how I feel, so live with it."

She rounded on him angrily. "I'm not going to stop my life just because you feel guilty."

"I never told you to stop your life, Hiroe. I just want to you wait for the right time."

"And you're the one who gets to decide *my* right time? Well, forget that. I'll just find a real boyfriend."

In two steps he was on her, hands on her upper arms.

"Don't do this to be vindictive. All that will happen is you'll wind up getting hurt."

"What do you care?"

Suddenly he turned and pressed her up against the stone wall of the temple. He had an arm on either side and a leg between both of hers. His lips were close and his breathing ragged. Hiroe struggled, aghast. No one could see them now, but someone could turn the corner at any moment.

"Listen!" he said forcefully, and she was compelled to stop moving. "Maybe it's not obvious to you, but I care quite a bit."

They stood that way with gazes locked. Out of the corner of her eye, Hiroe could see the cherry blossoms falling to the avenue, just a few steps away.

"You want it your way?"

"It's not—"

"Do you want it your way?!"

"If that's how you see it, then yes!"

"Fine. Meet me at the temple after school."

He walked off without looking back. Hiroe gazed after him, confused, her throat tight with words that had gotten stuck. The event had to be some kind of victory, yet it didn't feel that way at all.

SHICHI

Naturally, her friends got to hear everything.

"Make sure he buys you something nice," said Asuka, playing the role of auntie. She was only a year older, yet well versed in this type of transaction. She'd given her virginity away on four separate occasions and had found it quite profitable.

"Quiet, you girls!" commanded their teacher, and of course there was no choice but to obey.

HACHI

"You want to give me my present?" whispers Hiroe.

"That's right." He sweeps a hand over the table's smooth, shiny surface. "Go on."

Hiroe gets up, adjusts the pleats of her skirt, and then sinks uncertainly down onto the black lacquer. He is still on his cushion, gazing up at her now. She blushes furiously.

He reaches up to stroke the tender flesh of one calf, to run his hand over her fashionably bunchy sock and slide it down to her ankles so he can kiss the smooth flesh he has laid bare. The other sock promptly follows, and when both her legs are naked, he begins kissing his way slowly up one and then the other, in careful increments calculated to tease. Whenever his lips reach a new level, he pauses long enough for her to draw a breath and then switches to the other leg, starting at the bottom and moving steadily up. At the level of her knees, he feels resistance. Her legs close in on either side of his head, forcing him away.

He sits back.

She's the very image of timidity, there on the table with her eyes closed and her head turned to one side. Her knees are together now and the last knuckle of her middle finger is pressed against her lips. It's almost a caricature, really, and John doesn't know which is stronger, his irritation or his mad urge to laugh.

"Come on. Don't tell me you're going to play the blushing maiden now, after all this."

Her eyes flutter open. "What?"

He sighs and looks smilingly ceiling-ward. "Amida Buddha, grant me the patience to—"

"Oh no you don't," she laughs, ending his prayer with a kiss.

When they finally come up for air, he grins at her. "Ah, there's my impetuous darling."

"I'm not impetuous."

"Of course you are," he says, kissing her knees. "And also predisposed to theatrical displays of hyperfemininity. But you're young and Japanese, so I'll forgive the second flaw."

"And the first?"

He grins. "You'll learn that in time. Want your present now?"

"Yes," she husks, making every effort to look at him directly.

"Then spread your legs."

He leans into her then, bunching her pleated skirt in his hands as his questing lips find the source of her secrecy. Her nether lips are held closed by a thin cotton veil and he kisses her though the white eyelets. A moment later he feels her begin to dissolve. Her legs relax on either side of him. Her hands sink into the pool of his wavy blonde hair, combing it out and stroking it as he licks her. The first touch of his tonguetip feels to Hiroe as if one of the cherry petals has alighted at the base of her mons, where the bud of her womanhood would jut if it weren't wrapped in cotton and imprisoned between the pouting lips of her sex. The next touch is a slow, broad stroke of his tongue along her dewy furrow. After two more strokes it's unclear how much of the dew is coming from within and how much from without. But the scent of her guides him. John breathes her in, filling himself with the scent that reminds him of an ocean breeze after the rains in late summer.

A dovelike sound from above encourages John to explore further. His licks are deliberate. No matter how she rolls her hips or presses into him, he keeps his own pace, nuzzling her stiffened bud or nibbling at her sweet lips or pointing his tongue and, only when she is no longer expecting it, pushing it into her cranny.

At last, a pause. He stops to watch her. She is adrift on a cloud-sea of pleasure, with her eyes closed, swaying gently on the table. Tenderly he collects Hiroe from her uncertain perch and gathers her into his arms. It is a sweet feeling to have her there, this warm, heavy, girl-shaped bundle with her temple pressed up against his chin.

He touches her cheek and she nuzzles, catlike, against his hand. He traces the outline of her lower lip—the very fullest, pinkest part. Her mouth opens and, fluidly, his thumb slides in. At the new sensation, her eyes open as well. They follow the path of his digit as he draws it away and glosses her lips with it. So he lets her have it back, and her eyes fall closed once more.

"That's a good girl. Suck it."

Another small sound escapes Hiroe. Her hands tighten on his knees.

"Suck. With that pretty mouth and those cheeks all hollow. Do you have any idea how many times you've shown up in my dreams like this, you little carp?"

She moans for real this time, wanting nothing more than for him to slide his hands down under her skirt, under everything, to touch the very core of her and finish what he has started. All those nights she had lain in her bed, with her own hands wandering through her garden, are nothing compared to the distilled essence of desire that is coursing through her now.

And so her need expresses itself in the movements of her lips. They close upon the narrow part of his thumb and he twists, enjoying the feeling of her tongue fluttering against its very tip— a heady sensation, even without her pert bottom pressed enticingly into his groin. Still, he knows Hiroe is expecting her gift, so he lets the digit pop free and uses his hands to slide her panties down. He tucks the hem of her skirt carefully into its waistband and gazes down at her from above, at her mound and the beautiful thatch of hair that graces it. Hiroe feels open and exposed, but the rustle of the paper bag distracts her.

He takes out an ordinary sea sponge, golden and no larger than his palm.

She wants to ask, tries to, but he shakes his head no, and the movement is transmitted along his jaw and through the obsidian waterfall of her hair. Her eyes trace every movement of the sponge, from the bag, in a low arc past the table, to the floor with its tray and teacups and kettle of water, no longer steaming, only warm. The kettle is as shallow as her breathing. It has a wide opening in the top, large enough for him to dip the entire sponge inside. He soaks it and squeezes just slightly. There is no other sound in the room, in the teahouse, or perhaps in the entire world.

Water is falling in drops now, from the sponge and onto her young and sensate skin. The first two drops, fat and rapid, alight on her stomach and splatter there. He goes back and squeezes out the sponge a little more. The next few drops are slower. They fall on her belly, her mons, and then on her pink and jutting center. She hisses at the teasing contact. She struggles to get free, beating her stockinged feet against the tatami. But his other arm is locked about her waist and there is no way to free herself without hurting him.

He waits, with the sponge in his upturned palm, until she is finished struggling. Then he turns his hand over and begins again.

The next drop falls exactly where he wants it, and so he braces his forearm against her bent knee and lets the sponge hover there as he watches the subtle interplay of gravity and tension. Hiroe is keening softly in his arms. He soothes her with murmured words. Nonetheless, each tiny impact makes her body jerk. Soon she is digging her nails into the long muscles of his thigh, and of the arm that binds her, her head rolling from side to side. He goes back for more water. Again he lets it drip against her core and again the struggle begins. But after a time, her breathing quiets down. He can feel her heart slowing and, in the tiny movements of her eyes, sense her attention wandering from the sponge between drops. The water is cool now, as it trickles along her slit to the sodden pillow beneath her. She cools as well, and her sighs are frustrated.

"What's the matter?"

"John, I—I don't think I can. . . . "

"Don't think you can what?"

"You know," she says shyly, half-turning to press her cheek into the row of buttons on his shirt.

"You can say it."

A sigh. "Come," she breathes at last. "I don't think I can come like this."

"Well, who said you were supposed to?"

She pulls away to look at him. "But—"

"But what?" he remarks, tenderly untucking her skirt and smoothing her hair into a semblance of order. "Oh, I see. You thought that due to the elegance of the surroundings I was going to, maybe, deflower you here?"

"I—"

"Or perhaps that this was all about your pleasure? That there wasn't something bigger wrapped up in all of this?" John regards her with a bemused expression as he squeezes out the last of the water and returns the sponge to its paper home.

"But . . . you want to." She reaches for that forbidden part of him, and at her delicate touch he springs instantly back to full erection.

"You," he says, pointedly removing her hand, "need to learn some patience."

She regards him with a dark, shifting kind of expression. "All this time I've waited for you and you're telling me I need to learn patience?"

"All these months of teasing me, you mean."

"Teasing you?" Her expression hardens and she chokes the words out, rising up onto her knees, small fists angled away from her body.

The instant stretches out into a moment and then into a longer time. The dim lighting along the floor etches years into her face and her frame trembles, but it is her eyes that finally enlighten. The pain in them—he'd never seen it before.

He opens his arms then. She is reluctant at first but then comes into that longed-for circle. A kiss and she trembles in every part. A hand beneath her skirt and she sighs. This time he goes directly to her slippery cleft, working her still-swollen nub with a trio of careful fingers until she gasps, until her hands tighten on his crisp, white sleeves and she coats him with her essence, at last turning to muffle her impassioned cries against his chest.

When her eyes blink open, he has another kiss for her, soft as a cherry blossom on the sacred space between her brows.

"Hiroe," he says at last. "I'm sorry. I promise—no more games."

So that when her small hand closes around the hardness that still pulses at the root of him, and when that member leaps in her hand like a fish, he surrenders, at last. ◆

THE UGLY COCK DANCE

BY MARY GAITSKILL

Mitchell and Michelle were a good-looking, middle-aged couple who were getting hairy in the wrong places and going to fat. Michelle was approaching menopause, which meant she couldn't sleep, couldn't remember things, meant her face broke out, that she was moody, meant her pussy felt sort of dry a lot of the time.

She would wake at 5:30 in the morning and sit next to Mitchell, staring out the window at their beautiful yard thinking hateful, despairing thoughts for hours. Either that or she would giddily leap up and go downstairs and clean the house, thinking, "I am coming into my power!" which would've been good except she couldn't think straight enough to do anything with it. After she finished cleaning she'd sit and stare and feel broad, wordless feelings surge through her body. Sun, air, furniture, paper, dust;

it all became monstrously corporeal and dense. She felt the molecular heaviness of it pressing in upon her while the force of her own blood and organs pressed out, mashing her between them. It used to be when she felt between her legs, her pussy felt alert and full of energy, unfurled like a hairy, sensate flower. When she checked it out now, it felt tentative, weak and blind, like the moles her cat used to drag in.

Today was Sunday, which meant she didn't have to go to work—Michelle was a senior editor for an online magazine—on no sleep. Instead she went out in the garden in her underwear, weeding and thinking about her past. She had been something of a hippie and a bon vivant in her youth, which somehow over time had gotten translated into "slut." Sometimes that was okay, sometimes not. Sometimes it was okay that she hadn't had a child, sometimes it wasn't. Sometimes thousands of voices would be arguing about it inside her. Today, a particularly loud voice was yelling "ugly cunt." Well, let it yell. Virtuously, she weeded. It was hot and muggy. It hadn't rained for days, and the dirt was too dry. Bugs and beetles crawled around, making everything seem complex and full of holes. She had arugula, lettuce, chard, garlic, and basil. Soon she would have tomatoes. Suddenly, it was unbearably heavy to her, all those things with their roots digging down. She got up and dragged the sprinkler out, stuck it in the dry center of the garden. She turned it on, and it threw a bright, festive arc of water that slapped her ankle as she went back inside.

Upstairs in the bedroom, Mitchell was having his own problems. He was realizing that while he would continue to make a good living doing portraits and weddings—selling his work in stores and galleries, as well as the occasional magazine—he would never be a famous photographer. He was realizing he would never be as strong as he used to be: when he lifted too much weight at the gym his back hurt. If he ate late at night, his stomach got gassy and gross. He could sleep, but when he woke up his wife was sitting there staring like a zombie, sometimes intoning weird, depressing things about moles. She hardly ever wanted to have sex anymore, which hurt his feelings. It used to be she always wanted to have sex. She would wake him up sucking his dick with nice slurping noises; she'd climb on top of him and sit on his penis, bracing herself with her hands on his chest and using her legs energetically. She liked it with him on top, too, frontward and from the back. She liked it when he grabbed her legs and pushed them over her head so he went as deep as he could go. Once when he did that, she raised up her head and chest and spread her arms wide like he was spreading her legs, popped open her eyes, and stuck her tongue all the way out like a sex demon while he fucked her.

Given this history, it was hard not to take her sudden withdrawal personally. They had been married only five years, and Mitchell was still romantic about Michelle. He was the kind of guy who was actually sort of excited by domesticity—just the phrase "my wife's asshole" was enough to get him going sometimes. He thought guys who lusted after younger women were an embarrassment, and when he fantasized, he almost always thought about doing something really dirty with Michelle. His imagination had room for enjoyable sidebars about faceless sluts

or the girl at the store with the big ass, but basically he was outrageously faithful. And because of this, Michelle's stark, staring
asexuality made him feel especially uncertain and self-question-
ing. It made him look in the mirror and think awful things.

That's what he was doing that morning when Michelle
walked in on him. Standing barefoot in shorts, sucking in his
stomach, thrusting out his chest, and tilting his head back with
his hands on his waist in a hopeful parody of arrogant pride, he
was actually thinking "I'm fat." Michelle threw him a sarcastic
glance.

"Stop being silly," she said, "you know it doesn't matter if men
put on weight." She had that bristling, coming-into-her-power
look, which, on the whole, he liked better than the ugly cunt/mole
thing. She opened the closet and stood in her panties and bra,
scanning its contents. Dirt from the garden was on her feet and
her butt, and she was a little sweaty. Her stomach was bloated in
that way it tended to be these days; it gave her otherwise pert figure an extra-nasty look that he rather liked. He did not feel the
same way about his love handles, which, as far as he was concerned, did too matter.

"It's horrible out," she said. "Humid and hot."

"Once," said Mitchell wistfully, "a woman looked at me and
said 'That's a nice piece of steak!' She said it loud enough for me
to hear her."

"That's sort of nice," she said absently, and it was; his voice
conveyed the woman's affable relish, the joyous animal feeling of
pouncing and eating in the refined form of a horny, good-natured
woman. Wonderful to be the cantering zebra that aroused this

leonine roar—wonderful to roll that feeling of eating and being eaten back and forth between you until it didn't matter who was doing which. She remembered it very well.

He dropped his hands and relaxed his stomach, letting it hang out. "I used to be a lithe young man," he said softly.

"And I used to be a pristine girl." Her tone was light, a little impatient. "Where's my fucking sundress?" She closed the closet and turned to face him. Frontally, her small waist gave her hips and thighs a blunt, slightly ursine look. He felt a burst of animal warmth pass between them and thought, "Maybe—"

"Even when I was a pristine girl, I was probably an ugly cunt. Even then." She turned away and began going through her drawers.

"Oh, goddammit," he thought. But what he said was "So? I was an ugly cock then, too. Stuffing it down every throat, up every cunt and ass."

She chuckled mildly and continued to paw through her drawer.

"Ugly cock," he thought. Weirdly, a little strain of music rose up around the words in his head, a sort of oafish, optimistic theme song, like something dwarves would dance to. He could just see them, marching single file, full of dirty purpose. Suddenly, it popped out of his mouth, three crude, happy syllables on an upswing: "Nah nah NAH!"

Still bent over, Michelle turned and regarded her husband, a matted curtain of bed hair hanging in her face. "What?"

"I think I need to do an ugly cock dance."

"A *what?*"

"Nah nah nah nah nah NAH!" He squatted slightly, put his hands in front of his crotch like he was jerking off a tree, and stumped around thrusting his hips, grunting tunefully.

She turned around and stood with her mouth open. Her husband was grimacing like a lewd troll! He was letting his stomach hang all the way out! He was cavorting like . . . like . . .

An ugly cunt dance: What would it look like?

Now Mitchell was standing sideways to her, sensually peeling his lips back to show his teeth as he rotated his hips like he was fucking a hippopotamus. "Nah nah nah!" he asserted.

It was like watching a member of a primitive tribe do a rain dance. It made no sense, it had nothing to do with your life, and it was stupid-looking—yet something in you would rise up in response. Without even knowing what it was, Michelle felt the ugly cunt dance coming on. As Mitchell locomoted across the room—thrusting his hips and bossily shaking them—she pulled her panties down to midthigh and reached down to daintily part her labia.

"La la la la la LA!" She sang the same tune, only instead of grunting, her noise was high and pungent as a glandular odor, foul and pretty as a little cat with a mole in its jaws. Mitchell turned to see her prancing across the room on her tiptoes, shoulders back, chin up, legs together, and cunt lips open as she prissily twitched her hips and la la–ed, her little red tongue gaily hitting the ridged roof of her mouth. He gave a bellow—"ahhh!"— a sound of animal rightness, even probity.

"Nah nah nah!" His syllables got blurry and focused at the same time, like somebody honing in on a bright, flashing target and letting everything else fall away. He strutted around behind her.

"La la LA!" She reached back to lift and spread her butt with both hands so he could see her pussy between her closed thighs plus her eggplant-colored asshole. "La!" That one little sound, so ladylike and dirty and smug! Still on her toes, she pranced ahead of him, into the middle of the room. Here was her youth, she thought, high-pitched and self-involved, parading itself as if it were special, not knowing it was everything ordinary in a fresh envelope. Ridiculous and beautiful in spite of itself.

She turned and there was Mitchell. There was his youth, clumsy and buoyant, all gross enthusiastic want, everything about him hanging out, his b.o. flying like a flag. He put both hands on his belly and rubbed, and suddenly, there was his middle age—the crude happiness of an animal with a comfortable stomach, rooting, snuffling, hairy belly wagging as he padded through the forest on his rough paws. Still on tiptoes, she spread her legs and squatted slightly, bringing her hands up front and moving them like she was stirring a pot. What was in the pot? Her voice got deep, guttural. All the sun and air and dirt. All the vegetables in her garden, the bugs and fungi eating leaves and flesh, the worms tunneling underground. The mournful earthen smells, musty and fresh at the same time. Slowness, heaviness, tenderness, wordlessness. She dropped down off her toes and danced in place with a humble flat-footed plod. This was her middle age. The dark pit opened, and inside it, all the slow heavy things of the earth seemed to move with sickening velocity: boulders, babies, skeletons, strings of intestines, heads of lettuce, the wicked witch on her bicycle. Bloody hearts cannonballed past, there was a storm of ovaries. Outside, thunder rumbled. Michelle laughed. This was her old age. Outside, it began to rain. Michelle put her hands over her eyes and laughed, standing still with her panties down and her bush sticking out.

Mitchell went to grab her—but before he could, she sank down on the bed and began to cry. Both of them were sweating slightly, and their skin stuck together as they embraced. He unfolded her and laid her down. She stopped crying and looked at him with young-girl eyes. She pulled the cups of her bra down so she could feel his hairy chest on her breasts. He unzipped his pants and breathed with little grunts as he worked them down, his weight on her for an awkward moment. The sound of the rain pulled her attention out the window; she had a feeling of dis-solving, like she was breaking up into sparkling gray dots and scattering. Then Mitchell pushed into her, bringing her back with the solid ka-chunk! of dick in cunt. And then they were in the dark flesh-pit, flying along with everything else.

When they were finished, they lay together on their sides, Mitchell embracing her from behind. He was not sleeping. He was deeply resting in his feelings of love and pleasure. Michelle was resting in her feelings, too. She was also listening to the rain. She imagined it hitting her garden, making rich mud and running rivulets. She imagined it pouring through her, breaking her up like a clod of earth. She imagined opening a door in the rain, stepping inside it and vanishing. She closed her eyes and slept. ◆

ON THE USES OF A BATHTUB

BY JEFFREY S. CHAPMAN

When Aunt Sally was almost dead my girlfriend and I went through her bungalow filtering forty years of collected items—some useless, some priceless—collecting anything that wasn't junk to be appraised by an antique dealer and sold, along with the house, to pay Sally's hospital debts. After a weekend of work we stood by the front door and looked at a living room and a dining room piled with cabinets, couches, chairs, lamps, and memorabilia from every era, primarily the fifties and sixties. Sunlight angled in through windows over the mantelpiece, catching all the dust kicked up in our efforts and lighting the wood and fabric of the furniture, warming it with the rich brass tone that appears only when the sun is low on the horizon. Trash was piled obesely by the curb, and on the porch lay a small pile of things we wanted to keep.

I wanted everything. I wanted old things that looked nice even if they didn't work anymore. Christina argued and vetoed all weekend, and we kept a few choice items only. A rack of clothing from the fifties and sixties: dresses and overcoats and a couple of Uncle Lou's dinner jackets, not quite too small to fit me. A stainless steel blender because we didn't have a blender. Two old Shaker-style chairs. Some records by dead crooners. Two boxes of books—Stendhal and Balzac and Agatha Christie—and an oak bookshelf.

"Done," I said. I wiped off my forehead with the sleeve of my T-shirt.

"Well done," Christina said.

"I hope Aunt Sally appreciates this," I said.

"I'm sure she would, if she wasn't dying."

"Death is no excuse for ingratitude."

"Who's doing this for gratitude?" She pointed to the pile on the porch. "I'm doing this for the Bing Crosby records."

"We're being crass again."

"I know," Christina said. "I'm sorry."

"Poor Aunt Sally."

Christina nodded. We liked Aunt Sally. She was actually my father's aunt, but everyone called her Aunt Sally. She was almost ninety.

"Did we forget anything?" I said.

She shook her head and we started moving our small pile from the porch to my truck. But as she was carrying the last box of books, Christina said, "Ah."

"What?" I said.

"I forgot one thing," she said.

"What?"

"The bathtub. Do you think we could take the bathtub?"

"Out of the bathroom?"

"Not that bathtub. The bathtub in the backyard."

I had no idea what she was talking about. So we walked around the house and, sure enough, there was a claw-foot bathtub back by the garage, half-hidden behind some dried-out sunflowers that were bigger than hubcaps. Now that I saw it I wasn't sure how I had ever missed it; I'd been to that house a hundred times. The tub was painted white and the underside was dirty. I saw, as I walked up, that it was holding various pots—a large strawberry pot and smaller flowerpots. The plants that had once been there had since dried out. It was acting merely as a pot for pots. An über-pot, as it were.

"We already have a shower," I said.

"But we don't have a bath. And this is an old bath. Look how deep it is. I've always dreamed of a deep, old bathtub." She reached into the bathtub to demonstrate how deep it was. I was fighting a battle I had no chance of winning.

She started pulling out the pots and scooping out dirt. She pointed to the hose and I turned it on. I thought about spraying her—it was still hot out—but I knew the retaliation would be brutal. I contented myself by spraying her feet twice. After five minutes of rinsing, we had it almost spotless. Infected by Christina's excitement, I didn't even think, until after we'd returned with friends to help load it into the truck, that bathtubs need plumbing; Christina probably thought about plumbing right away but never mentioned it to me, not wanting to give me cause for objection.

It sat in one corner of the spare bedroom, opposite the futon. I'd wanted to put our new bookshelf there, but it ended up in the living room instead. We moved my desk to our bedroom. I'm flexible. It seemed impossible to get plumbing to the tub and equally impossible to fit the tub somewhere where there was plumbing. For a while Christina would sit in the bathtub with a book and pretend to be taking a bath. The surface of the tub was shockingly cold. She would put a plug in the drain before she sat in the tub, and when she was done she'd pull the plug. I'd lie on the futon and she'd read to me. If she was feeling charitable, or hot, she'd strip down before stepping in. Sometimes she'd strip to her undershirt and cotton panties, sometimes she took off the top as well. If I tried to climb in she'd stop me; a palm on my forehead pushed me back. The tub was her space. I'd retreat to the futon and sometimes, sometimes, she would follow me out, straddle me, sit on me. I would run fingers along her waist, up her stomach, under her breasts, along her clavicle—a paper-thin touch. Best was the skin on the insides of her arms; more smooth and soft than anything else I can imagine. I loved sliding a finger into her, pressing against her belly from inside, gesturing come-hither until she came. We fucked a lot in that room: sitting on the futon, leaning against the wall, on the floor next to the bathtub. Never *in* the bathtub.

It was a summer of record heat in Salt Lake City: two weeks straight of over one hundred degrees, dry heat and blue skies. We had a swamp cooler—that brought it down to the high eighties inside—and we didn't want to go out much. We started drinking lemonade, or gin and tonics. We drank lemonade directly from our new blender and sat out on the porch with books until the sun went down and the mosquitoes came out. Christina would raise the blender and toast Aunt Sally.

August drew to an end and the temperature dropped into the nineties. Aunt Sally's house was sold for much more than anyone expected. We bought a citronella so we could sit out on the porch at night and watch for heat lightning, but we used it only twice before Christina's school started again—she was in her first year of a master's degree in nursing—and although we said we would try to make time to relax and sit, we didn't. She was busy. She was gone all day and most evenings; she was either in class, or at the hospital, or in the library studying. If she was at home she was likely sleeping. She started going to bed at nine o'clock if she was home. Once I came home at six in the evening to find the record player playing static, the needle having come to the center. Christina was sleeping in a chair, with a book in her lap. I woke her up, and she said she must have fallen asleep before three.

"All the death and dying wears me out," she said, smiling.

I had taken off the summer after graduation, and when Christina went back to school, I found a job. I worked as a waiter at a diner, taking as many morning or afternoon shifts as possible, so I could write and read in the evening. I moved my desk back into the spare bedroom—we never had guests—so I could work after she'd gone to sleep. There was hardly enough space for the desk and the bathtub and all my books, which I would wedge and stack wherever I could. If I had had my way I would have thrown out the tub: I knew we'd never get around to hooking up the damned thing. I thought about suggesting it, but it would have made her mad and worn out. So instead I bought some boards, laid them over it and used it as a table for my books. Christina may not have noticed. She never mentioned it to me.

She didn't ask me about my writing at all that winter.

The summer had been warmer than average and the winter was colder than average, as if Newton's law of equal and opposite reactions had a climatic equivalent. November was cold and snowy; more so than any November in my memory. The clouds lay low, making the days especially gray and constrictive. Toward the end of November I was vacuuming the living room when Christina walked through the front door, chewing her fingernails. Her eyebrows angled down as if she was questioning something.

I switched off the vacuum. She looked at me, bemused.

"It's cold, isn't it," she said.

"Yeah," I said.

"I mean *really* cold, right?"

"Yeah. Super cold."

"Good. It's not just me," she said. She chewed on her thumbnail. "Because I'll tell you . . . I'm always cold these days. Even when I wear two sweaters."

"It's cold these days. You're also stressed out and worn down—you're always studying. That'd make anyone cold."

"It's all the disease," she said. "So much disease. Death has long, chilly fingers."

She went into the kitchen and I was left with the ominous image of the Grim Reaper wrapping his hands around her. I'd never known Christina to be troubled by sickness and disease. She'd been relaxed about it. Casual. She'd rarely mentioned her cases. At most she would crack a joke about a patient with genital warts or the hypochondriac who came to the ER every week. Now, over meals, she was telling me about motorcycle accidents or children with chronic diseases.

We hardly ever had sex anymore. Instead I masturbated a lot, thinking about how Christina looked in her tight cotton underwear, picturing her breasts, her small dark nipples, the ring in her belly button, the curve of her ass. I remembered how she looked the first time we had sex, the position of her body and the look on her face, not when she came but before—the relaxed and focused look she had when we fucked.

My fantasies usually focused on specific memories. I loved thinking about how she took control in our sex life. She was the bolder of us. For example: early one afternoon we stood leaning our elbows on the kitchen counter, talking about what happened with our days. I put on coffee. She told about the routine doctor's checkup she'd been at. Suddenly, brassily, she took a piece of paper out of her bag, unfolded it, and slid it toward me. It was a page with suggestions for "10 New Sex Positions for the New Year" that she'd ripped from a women's magazine in the doctor's office. She pointed to one drawing and said, "I want you to do this." It was two o'clock—I was a more traditional, sex-after-dark guy—but she was already hiking up her skirt and raising her eyebrows. She lay face down, on the carpet in the living room and I was left with little option. I knelt down, pulled her panties down across her thighs. Her ass was smooth and sculpted. I slipped a finger between her legs: she was impossibly wet. I unzipped my pants and entered her from behind while she lay flat, legs and stomach pressed flat against the carpet. The angle made everything feel tighter than usual, and Christina pushed back against me, excited. She was so wet. That's what I remember—how wet she felt.

These days I really wanted to have sex like we did before, but she was too tired, too tired. Maybe tomorrow. So I stopped asking. Every night I pressed up to her when I came to bed, but she was a deep sleeper.

Aunt Sally died in early December, toward the end of Christina's semester. My dad called one night, late, after I'd come home from work, while Christina and I were having a pre-bedtime decaf; she was trying to convince me that she was going to fail out of school.

My dad told me that Aunt Sally had died, and I hesitated a moment before telling Christina. She started to cry. She cried harder than I've ever seen her cry; so hard that I, too, started.

After a while she said, "At the hospital you manage to hold the sadness at bay because you don't know the patients. It's different when you know someone.

"There are two inevitabilities in life," she continued, smiling a wan smile. "Death and exams."

"I thought it was taxes," I said. She shook her head and pulled her cardigan closer.

A bitter wind whipped down from the canyons when she

went off to school the next morning. It couldn't have been more than nine degrees out with windchill.

She will want to be warm, I thought. *Blankets? Tea? The bathtub. Yes. Sturdy, deep, covered with books.*

I filled pots—one large soup cauldron, two medium pots, and a teakettle—and set them to boil an hour before she was due home. I removed my books and boards from the bathtub and put towels on the floor. By the time she came home I had emptied boiling water from the smaller pots four times and from the large pot twice. There was about seven inches of water in the bathtub. Seeing four pots on the stove, she said, "Are you making dinner?"

I smiled and shook my head. I gave her a kiss. "How was school?" I asked.

Her eyes were half-closed and her strawberry hair was pulling loose from the ponytail she had made. She had thrown her coat directly over her scrubs. She smiled, but it seemed halfhearted.

"Long," she said. "And hard."

"I have a treat for you," I said.

"Not dinner?"

"No."

I grabbed the large pot with two pot holders and led her into the spare room. There were no candles, no music, no special lights, just the bathtub with seven inches of water. She stood for a minute, bemused, and then she felt the water.

"A little lukewarm," she said. I poured in the large pot.

"Get in," I said. "I'll keep it warm."

"How are you going to empty it?"

"I don't know. We'll see."

I went back to the kitchen, refilled the empty pot, and checked on the other pots of water. They were close to boiling, close enough. I took two with me; Christina had already shed her scrubs and wrapped a towel around herself. She looked amused. I poured in the two pots and she tested it with her toe. She pulled it back. "Hot," she said.

She lowered herself in while I returned those pots to boil. I came back and she was lying low in the bath, almost up to her neck in water, pale breasts blotching red with the heat. Her eyes were closed. I turned off the light and lay down on the futon.

"Life goes on," I said. "Tests or no tests."

She laughed.

"True," she said. It was steamy and dark and I, too, closed my eyes and relaxed. ◆

THE
FLOOD

BY J. HARTMAN

J ames and Margaret Dawson came home to Los Robles Valley
in the early dusk. They had to walk over the pass from Forest
Hills, through the woods; they couldn't use the road, because
men from the Army Corps of Engineers were guarding it. In the
morning, the new dam would go into operation, and Los Robles
Valley would become Los Robles Reservoir.

James and Margaret didn't speak as they walked. James
glanced over at Margaret every now and then. She always had her
eyes on the ground, picking out her steps, avoiding the twigs and
stones. Her dark brown hair was pulled back in a severe bun that
made her look forty instead of twenty-four. Her clothes . . . She
never complained, but James knew she wished they could afford
something nice once in a while. Maybe they could use some of the
government money from the house, from the relocation, for a new
dress. Hard times. If he'd been laid off from the lumberyard
sooner, he might've gotten a PWA job, working on the dam. . . .

At last they came to the little house at the end of Aldercroft Lane. It looked bare, barren. The flowers in the front yard had been trampled; the shutters on the front window were broken. The front door stood ajar.

They hadn't bothered to take all of their things with them when the Corps had forced them to sell the house and land. They'd figured on making a fresh start in Los Perros.

But Margaret had insisted that they come back. "Just for tonight," she'd said. "One last night." Her chin had been high, her face impassive. The same stony mask she'd worn ever since. . . .

James held the door for her, even though it was already open. *Useless,* he thought. *What am I doing here? What are* we *doing here?*

Margaret looked around in the gloom of the front hall. James unclipped a flashlight from his belt, flicked it on, handed it to her. He took off his hat, moved to hang it from the hat rack, remembered they'd sold the hat rack with the rest of the furniture. He hung the hat from a doorknob. He lowered his heavy rucksack—bedrolls, a little food—to the floor, leaned it against the wall.

Margaret stood uncertainly, shone the light across a wall covered in now-grimy floral wallpaper. She took a step toward the living room, then stopped, turned around, and walked into the kitchen.

James imagined the floodwaters rising, coming in through the front door, covering the wooden floor here in the front hall, muddying the wallpaper. He imagined the water filling the house, filling the valley, suffocating.

Margaret gave a little shriek. James darted through the doorway into the kitchen and stopped dead behind her.

A tall narrow man stood in the doorway between the kitchen and the dining room. A dirty tramp, tattered, filthy; he squinted and averted his eyes as the light hit him squarely in the face. He had several days' growth of beard. His clothes were old and torn; his hat was battered and, like the rest of him, caked with dirt.

James started forward. By God, nobody was going to come into his house, walk around like he owned the place. "What the—" He glanced at Margaret. "What do you think you're doing here?"

The man had put up a grimy hand, blocking the light from his eyes. "Sorry," he said. "I thought this place was— I'll leave. Sorry." His voice was quiet but clear.

James said, "Get out." His fists were balled at his sides. *Say something, say anything, and I'll hit you, I swear to—*

"Wait," said Margaret. She shifted her flashlight a little so it wasn't directly in the hobo's face. "Don't you know they're going to flood the whole valley in the morning?" she said. "It isn't safe here."

The man looked at them, a flash of curiosity brightening his eyes, but then looked away. "I know," he said. "Just hoping there was some food left behind, maybe something soft to sleep on tonight before I move on. But— Sorry to intrude." He started past them. Margaret stepped aside to let him pass; James stood his ground. The man turned sideways to pass James and go through the doorway.

"Wait," said Margaret again. James glared at her. The other man stopped, still looking at the floor. Pausing for a moment before moving his heavy load on out of there.

"What's your name?" Margaret asked.

"Cody," said the man. "Richard Cody." He glanced up, side-long, past James at Margaret, then down again. "They call me Professor," he offered. "Down at the jungle by the train yard."

"Look, just—" James began, but Margaret cut him off.

"Cody," she said. "Mr. Cody, the pump in the back should still work. If you go clean yourself up, I'll see if I can make the—the guest room a little more comfortable."

When Cody was gone, James said, "He's a bindlestiff, Margaret. Like as not slit our throats as we sleep."

"He's a man in trouble, James Dawson." She glared at him. He looked away, tight-lipped. She said, "Go make yourself use-ful—go out to the shed and see if you can find any of those jars of preserves. I think I might have left some behind."

* * *

James returned with a jar of preserved peaches he'd found under some timber in the shed.

With his face and hair washed, in a worn old nightshirt of James's that Margaret had found in the bottom of the closet, the hobo looked almost presentable. He'd somehow managed to shave. He had a nice firm jaw and keen blue eyes.

He gobbled peaches from the jar with his fingers, and some of the beef jerky James had brought along for breakfast. The man kept a wary eye on James and Margaret as he ate.

None of them said much. When the man was done, Margaret showed him to the guest room.

James and Margaret bedded down on the floor in their old

bedroom. James reached for Margaret, but she turned her back to him. Again. He lay restlessly for a while, but the day had worn him out, and eventually he slept.

*   *   *

He woke to the sound of sobbing.

Margaret wasn't lying next to him. He stood, still sleep-fuddled, and drew on his trousers. He buttoned the suspenders as he walked unsteadily down the hall in the darkness.

The sound was coming from the living room; he paused just outside the living room doorway. Moonlight splashed in through the big front window. Margaret was there; it was Margaret who was crying. Margaret who hadn't shed a tear for six months, Margaret who—

There was someone else in the room.

Two figures, sitting on the floor, backs to the wall, in the moonlight: Margaret was clutching the tramp, and he had his arms around her.

James took one step through the doorway, raising a fist, preparing a bellow that would shake the roof, would make the hobo take to his heels. He'd had about enough—

Margaret was still wailing, in great gasping sobs.

And the hobo was . . . comforting her? He was holding her, encircled in his arms, and he was saying soothing nonsense, *There, there,* and he had no right, no right at all—

But the tears, the grief, were flooding out of Margaret, finally released. That stone face had collapsed. James hadn't been able to reach her, hadn't been able to help; he'd stood by, helpless, useless, watching her, waiting, praying that one day she would come through that valley. . . .

But not like this. Not with another man. James stepped farther into the room. "You—" he tried, but he didn't know how to go on. "What are—"

The man looked up. His eyes widened in guilty fear; he pulled half away from Margaret but couldn't extricate his arms from around her. Margaret looked up, bewildered, and saw James.

The anguish on her face was more than he could bear. He moved toward her, reflexively, forgetting everything else. She put her arms out to him, and he sank to his knees and enfolded her in his own arms. And she continued to cry, onto his shoulder now.

James felt a slight motion, and looked up, and realized that the hobo—Cody—was still caught, his arms pinned around Margaret by the wall and by James's arms. James began to shift, to give Cody room to pull away and clear out, but Margaret, still crying, moved one of her arms, drew Cody in closer. Cody gave James an embarrassed half-shrug.

They sat there, awkwardly, the three of them, as Margaret cried herself out.

And then, as the sobs died away into hiccups, Margaret looked up at both of them and half-smiled through the tears. And then she kissed James.

It was so sudden, after all these months, that James didn't respond at first. When after a moment he did respond, it was as though his whole body was waking up from a sleep.

Margaret sank down to lie on the old rug. She pulled James down next to her, kissing him, stroking his head. "James," she said. "James, I need you." The urgency in her voice brought him fully erect. He pulled her to him—and stopped. The other man was still there.

Cody was pulling away, standing up. "I'll—ah—I'll just leave you to—"

But Margaret said, once again, "Wait." And sat up, and looked back and forth, from Cody to James and back again.

Both men froze in place. Guarded. Wary. Uncertain.

Margaret held a hand up to Cody. "Please," she said. "You too. Let's—be alive. Together. This one night, before the morning."

James's eyes narrowed. He drew in a breath—but Margaret put her finger to his lips. Her eyes caught his, pleading. "For me?" she said. "For—I need this. To—to prove I'm alive." James lay there, looking up at her, and past her at the other man. "Please?" she said, and he thought his heart would break.

A long moment passed.

At last, James half-nodded. If this was the price of getting Margaret back. . . . "Once," he said. "Tonight only."

She nodded. "Tonight only," she said.

Cody, beyond her, chuckled softly. "For a limited run," he said wryly, and somehow that was funny, and they all laughed, and then before anyone could say anything more, Margaret was standing and unbuttoning her nightgown, there in the white moonlight, and her dark hair was loose, cascading over her shoulders. It took James's breath away.

Margaret shrugged out of the shoulders and sleeves, and the nightgown slithered down her pale body.

Her breasts were still fuller than they'd once been, and there were wrinkles on her belly. But in the moonlight James could see echoes of the girl he'd courted, at the county fair that summer, back before the Crash, before everything had turned sour.

He was filled with a fierce need to take her, right there, heedless of the stranger in the room. He stood, reached for her. She danced back a step, a half-smile playing around her lips. It had been so long since he'd seen her smile. . . . He lunged forward, grabbed her. He managed somehow to lay her down on the floor, as she laughingly protested. He knelt beside her, fumbling with his suspender buttons, trying to get his trousers down.

And then Cody was beside them, kneeling on the floor. "You're lovely, ma'am, if you don't mind my saying so," he said. His voice was still quiet, but teasing now, challenging, questioning.

Margaret pulled the man down to her, kissed him. Jealousy flared in James. He managed to get his trousers down around his ankles, and lay down and pushed Cody away from her. He leaned in and kissed her himself. A long kiss, to make her forget the other man. What could she want from him? And after a moment, Margaret began to kiss back more urgently, and to make little noises in the back of her throat. He felt a moment of satisfaction, then confusion as the noises grew louder—she couldn't possibly be enjoying a few kisses quite that much—

He shifted, looked up. Cody was down between Margaret's legs, and his head was bobbing up and down at her groin. . . .

James broke away from the kiss. "That's disgusting," he said. Cody paused, looked up at him, raised an eyebrow. But before Cody could say anything, Margaret grabbed his head with one hand and shoved it down there again.

"That's . . . ," said James, but he knew when he was beaten. He shook his head. If this was what she really wanted. . . .

He guessed it was time for him to go. He would leave Margaret here, with—

She grabbed him and pulled him in for another kiss. A deep, passionate one. She moaned around it.

James remembered other times when she'd moaned, nights in the bedroom when their passion had made her scream with pleasure. The thought aroused him again.

He shifted an arm and began to stroke her breast. He'd learned she liked that. She responded, moving to press against his hand. Her moans into his mouth grew louder, her breathing faster.

James risked breaking the kiss long enough to glance down her body. The other man's head was still moving there. James lay perfectly still for a long moment, hand frozen on Margaret's breast, and then slowly moved his head. He paused again with his mouth an inch from the dark bud that tipped her breast, then reached with his tongue to touch it.

Margaret gasped and arched her back. James licked again, more firmly this time, and then, gathering his courage, took her nipple into his mouth.

Margaret screamed, head back, body convulsed. For a moment James thought he had somehow hurt her terribly, but then her hand was behind his head, clutching him to her breast. He sucked and licked at it, struggling to breathe through his nose, and then she went limp.

All was still for a moment. Then James pulled away from the awkward position Margaret had pulled him into, sat up a little.

Cody's head came up. He was grinning, and his mouth and chin were wet as if from eating ripe fruit. He wiped the back of his hand across his mouth and said to James, "You oughtta try it sometime."

James looked down at Margaret. Her eyes were closed; her mouth held an expression of perfect bliss. Two of her fingers rested gently against the other nipple, the one James hadn't touched.

James swallowed. His trousers were still tangled around his ankles; he pulled them the rest of the way off. He was erect, insistent. He shivered.

Cody, standing, stripped off his nightshirt. Without clothing, he was thin and pale. *Probably never worked a day in his life,* James thought. James touched his own arm—the hard muscles from wrangling lumber all day for ten years—and smiled a little to himself.

Margaret opened her eyes. "More?" she whispered.

"I—" James's mouth was suddenly dry. He swallowed. "I want you," he said.

She understood. She drew him down to her, pulled him close.

He tried to lie on top of her, but she turned on her side, away from him. *What—*

She reached back, pulled him close up against her back. And then lifted her upper leg and reached with one hand to guide him in from behind, to guide him home. She was slick and wet, and James tried not to think about Cody's mouth down there, his tongue licking. She was tighter than usual from this angle. It felt strange not to be facing her, not to be lying atop her as he thrust into her. He reached around in front of her and caressed her breast;

his other arm had somehow ended up trapped under her neck, immobile. Inside her, he moved slowly at first, trying to take things slow, to savor the moment, but he was going to have to speed up any second now, as she began to push back against him—

And then Cody was there. Lying on his side too, facing Margaret and James. He kissed Margaret and then shifted down to nuzzle her breasts. She gasped again, and began to moan. Her back pressed harder against James as she took him even deeper inside. James lost control, slamming hard into her, and was only vaguely aware that Cody had moved again and was lying full-length against her front, thrusting against her as if he, too, were entering her, only he was holding himself with one hand. They all rocked together, back and forth, faster and faster, as Margaret's keening wail went up and up and up, and with one final thrust James felt himself spurting deep inside her, his body hit by one jolt after another, and she was still screaming and bucking, and then James's hand on Margaret's breast was spattered by something sticky, and Cody grunted once and lay still.

And Margaret's breathing slowed into ragged gasps, and James realized sleepily that she was crying again. Not the body-shaking sobs of before, just quiet weeping. And both men had their arms around her, and James wasn't sure which of them said "It's okay, it's all right" and which said "It'll be all right, don't you cry."

And slowly her tears tapered off, and her breathing slowed, and then she was asleep.

James raised his head slightly, a little befuddled, uncertain. Cody looked him in the eyes from a couple of feet away. Cody quirked the corner of his mouth, a little sadly, and then leaned in to kiss Margaret gently on the forehead, and then he pulled away and sat up.

He looked at James again and said, in that quiet voice, "Margaret told me about your loss. I'm sorry."

James blinked back unmanly tears and bit his lip. "They moved the graves," he said. "The PWA men. All the graves, they moved them to higher ground. All but one."

Cody was silent for a moment, then said, "I think I'd best be going now. I—" He stopped and stood up. The moonlight was still bright on his skin.

James almost said, "Stay." But caught himself.

"Tonight only," Cody said. "I'll find somewhere else to sleep. I— Thank you. And thank her, in the morning."

"Thank you," James said, unsure even as he said it why he was saying it.

"Take good care of her," Cody said. He seemed about to say something more but thought better of it. He picked up the nightshirt he'd been wearing and disappeared through the doorway into the hall.

James thought about going after him. About thanking him, or hitting him, or something—he wasn't sure what he wanted to do. But before he could figure it out, he was asleep, still embracing his wife.

* * *

The birds outside woke them in the predawn gray. Margaret stretched and yawned, and smiled. James's heart thudded hard for a moment—her smile had always been one of his favorite things. Neither of them said much as they dressed and ate a little beef jerky.

When they were ready, hand in hand, they went out into the backyard and over to the oak tree.

Underneath it, propped up in the dirt, was a piece of cardboard. A pencil scrawl read:

James Dawson, Jr.
1935

Margaret squeezed James's hand tighter, and he moved to stand behind her, to put his arms around her. They both cried a little then.

And then the sun came up. The dam would be going into operation soon, flooding the valley, covering up old hurts, washing away the past, making everything clean and new again. It was time to go. ◆

SLICK

BY JACK MURNIGHAN

Hydrophobic, gynophobic, spermaphobic, and bespectacled, Elias Martin was not a prime candidate for love. Nor, in fact, had he had any brushes with Cupid's affliction, at least beyond his singular and lifelong passion for chemistry. He loved chemistry, its elements, laws, and, specifically, the periodic table. The natural elements, barring unstable radioactive isotopes, were, thought Elias Martin as early as the tender age of eleven, tidy, predictable, and marvelously mapped. It was a great moment in Elias Martin's boyhood when he first heard of Dmitri Mendeleev plotting out his famous table, how the Russian was unstalled by the absence of elements to fit every space on the chart. Instead of giving up on his scheme or changing his theory, Mendeleev concluded, ostentatiously, that there were elements that had not yet been discovered—and that he could name their characteristics. In time, Mendeleev was proven right; once he described how these undiscovered elements were going to be, it was much easier to find them. Elias Martin had long ago concluded that his life partner was a similar kind of element: undiscovered but very describable. And until she came along, he would remain as inert as argon.

Now thirty-one years old, Elias Martin worked as the head of a chemistry lab attempting to create new industrial lubricants. He and his team had managed to synthesize new forms of liquid polyurethane but had failed to find any that would generate the slipperiness necessary for the contracting company. Elias was becoming acutely frustrated; he had successfully performed his experiments, but not received the expected results. His assistants had no new ideas, and Elias Martin was feeling stymied. It was time to bring in another researcher.

It appeared to Elias Martin that the response he received to the ad he placed in the journal *Polymer,* announcing the position in his lab, must have been written the very day the publication left the presses. It was an email from an about-to-be graduate of Cal Tech, an honors student in chemistry with impeccable recommendations and a seemingly limitless interest in lubrication dynamics. Her cover letter went on and on: the research she did comprising her honor's thesis, the experimental approaches she wanted to pursue. She seemed to have promising, original ideas— just what the lab needed. The only problem was, she was a woman. Abigail Theresa Henderson, Phi Beta Kappa. She would be perfect for the job, if only she were not a she.

Elias Martin had never been comfortable with women—truth be told, apart from chemistry, he had never been comfortable with anything. And now he had to decide whether to let a woman into his lab. He had never worked beside a woman in this or any other lab, and had avoided any place that had a woman present. He steered clear of chemistry classes in college that had too many women in them, for fear of being paired off with one for projects, and since then he had not taken a job if it meant that he would have to research side by side with a woman. Elias Martin was in a bind, but in a moment of rare heroism, he decided it was time to attempt to be rational and conquer his fear. Elias Martin was unable to remember ever having conquered a fear. Oh, except taking the job in this lab in the first place. Yes, working with lubricants gave him the willies, but at least they were better than water. He had done it once, he concluded, and it was time to conquer his fears again.

What is fear? Elias Martin asked himself. Fear is a residual, atavistic weakness left over from man's connection to the animal kingdom. In some cases, of course, fear is prudent, but these tend to be referred to as caution. Fear, groundless fear, was a force of the unruly, ugly side of Nature—the part not nicely ordered by chemistry and physics. It was bad Nature, and up to Man to fight back.

Elias Martin knew that he was afraid of a number of things, as was everyone, but in particular he knew his fears of water and sperm were somewhat unusual, and was rather embarrassed about them. The fear of water was easy to explain, at least to some extent: his mother said she once put him in too hot a bath when he was very little. As to sperm, well. . . . He did not like to think back to the day he discovered sperm, or, more pointedly, was himself discovered as sperm was discovered. He had not known he was masturbating, did not yet know the abhorred term nor even what he considered the similarly abhorrent practice. He was but ten years old, seventy-two pounds, almost four years before the first hair graced his untended pubis. It was past his bedtime, and Elias Martin had turned in some half an hour before. His hand had made its way somehow between his legs, there was a pleasant sensation, one thing led to another, the pleasant sensation got more and more pleasant, and then . . . He refused to think about it and, from that day forward, never looked his mother in the eye again.

And pleasure—what is pleasure? Elias Martin knew less of pleasure than of fear; the one he had not encountered, the other he did not comprehend. And while Elias Martin recognized that bringing the young Ms. Henderson into his lab would put him face-to-face with his fears, he had no idea just how close it would bring him to the other of his great unknowns.

* * *

Abigail Henderson was a chemistry prodigy, and a very lonely young woman. From earliest childhood she had demonstrated an enormous scholastic aptitude, and by the age of eight she had focused all her attention on math, the sciences, and chess. Such an early and complete dedication to academic studies would have ostracized almost any young American; the fact that Abigail was a girl made it that much worse. By the time she entered high school, she could say with impunity that her only friends were her teachers, and they also had the honor of being the objects of all her fantasies.

It is not uncommon, as we all know, for students to develop crushes on their teachers; by and large, these crushes emerge when the instructor is still of remotely dateable age and attractiveness, and the thought of an affair has at least minimal credibility. In Abigail's unfortunate case, however, her crushes were based on no physical grounds whatsoever; they were purely intellectual and thus paid little heed to age differences as large as sixty-five years. The result, of course, was that while one party was rhapsodizing dreams of a melding of minds, the other was laughing no small number of patronizing chuckles at the outlandishness of a schoolgirl's fixation. This resulted in any number of explanatory conversations, each unspeakably painful to young Abigail. She, like Othello, loved, though loved not wisely, and found herself at the age of twenty-one completing a combined bachelor's and master's of science, never having had her feelings reciprocated.

Another matter complicated things, one that would eventually have everything to do with Abigail's selected course of study. Ever an avid reader, the adolescent Abigail made do with her lack of human affection by extensive (some would say compulsive) consumption of erotic literature. Pink romance novels, intellectually quite beneath her, were read furtively by taper and then hidden beneath her bed. She would eventually evolve to reading Victorian erotica, purchased from a specialty bookseller downtown, as well as classical and medieval sex manuals from China and the Near East. Her collection bloomed; the box beneath the bed was ever in danger of overflowing, and all the while Abigail Henderson was becoming extremely proficient in the fine art of self-stimulation.

But there was a catch: not all was as it should be. She had always suspected that something was amiss in her physiology; she had read, time and again, of the wetness and self-moistening of the vagina, of the sliding in and out of the male member, of women "growing damp" or "gushing"; she understood the poetic impulse toward amplification, and yet something did not jibe. In all her acts of self-love, the entirety of her apparatus remained dry as a Triscuit. She could give herself pleasure, yes, but she was invariably constrained to make use of lotions or lubricants, the tub or showerhead, a pool, the ocean, or a drop of saliva. The simple truth was that Abigail Henderson could not get wet, and by the time this was confirmed by a medical professional, Abigail had known it herself for years.

No surprise, then, her singular dedication to the science of lubrication. Abigail Henderson had concluded to take matters into her own hands, as she had done for so long. She read up on her phenomenon and found that other women were in the same dry-docked boat as she. And so Abigail Henderson had made it her private, personal mission to create the perfect incarnation of slickness, not so slippery as to lose the necessary feel and friction, not so clingy as to stick, slow, or gum. In short, she wanted to reproduce the natural function of the aroused human vagina, if not improve upon it, and she would harness the totality of science to bring about her goal.

The job in Elias Martin's lab was ideal to her purposes. Her professors at Cal Tech had encouraged her research into fluid dynamics, but none were experts in the field, and she had been unable to bring about the results she thought possible. Elias Martin was about to offer her the chance she was looking for, and, if the stars decided to align themselves properly, that chance would not be limited to the test tube. . . .

* * *

Her first day at the lab, Abigail Henderson began, without even realizing she was doing it, to turn the place on its ears. The other members of Elias Martin's team took to Ms. Henderson immediately. Her intelligence and good nature impressed them all, and her beauty, muted as it was by conservative dress, over-sized spectacles, the buttoning of even the top button of her blouse, and Abigail's complete ignorance or indifference to its potential, was nonetheless lost on no one. No one, not even Elias Martin. And yet he was unable to get over his basic, knee-jerk fear of her.

Abigail, over the years, had had such an effect on any number of her male colleagues, but, as in previous cases, interpreted it not as testament to her female charms, but as a sign that her intellect was not adequate enough to make her worthy in their eyes. The fact, of course, was quite the reverse. It was precisely her intellect that both appealed to and intimidated the male scientists, making them all the more susceptible to her beauty. This never would have occurred to Abigail Henderson.

Little would have changed in the present situation, were it not for two determining events: Abigail's twenty-second birthday, and a breakthrough at the lab. Both occurred on the same day, and what a magic day it was.

Three days before Christmas, six months after Abigail had started at the lab, she took the morning off to celebrate her birthday with her mother, who wanted to take her for a half-day at a beauty spa. It began with a salt rub, followed by a seaweed facial, an hour-and-a-half full-body massage, a manicure, pedicure, hair coloring, cut, and style. Abigail was resistant at first; she had an experiment in progress at the lab that she hoped would finally give them the lubricant they were looking for, and didn't want to take the time away. Furthermore, going to a spa didn't really fit with Abigail's self-image. But the massage felt good, the facial was exhilarating, her nails looked perfect, and when she looked in the mirror after her hair had been treated, tinted, and redone, she didn't recognize who she saw. She felt an emotion she had a hard time recognizing: pride. Now, looking in a mirror of the town's most expensive beauty salon, Abigail Henderson began to see herself as men saw her. And at that moment, she decided to speak to Elias Martin.

*　*　*

On her way to the lab to confront Elias, Abigail Henderson remembered her experiment. Her heart started racing; it should be completed by now. Everything she had imagined was finally being put to the test. This was the big one.

By the time she arrived at the lab, she had completely forgotten about speaking to Elias. She had also forgotten about her new hair, her makeup, the dress her mother had given her for her birthday, and the red polish on each of her twenty nails. She entered from the side door, as always (Elias had positioned her workstation next to the door; his was across the lab by the front), and went straight to her desk, not even hearing the gasps and "oohs" of her lab mates. While they were still taking in the vision of the new Abigail Henderson, she let out a scream. It had happened: the experiment had worked; she had found the breakthrough. She called for Elias in the very voice of elation.

Everything, everything she had worked for. When Elias arrived, she couldn't help but throw her arms around his neck. "Elias! Elias! We did it!" He would have been happy, he really would have been, if only she weren't touching him.

*　*　*

Elias Martin was at the fulcrum of two very different sets of stimuli. There was Abigail's new data, incontrovertibly the success they had been looking for. And then there was Abigail herself, looking radiant. She was ecstatic, beaming, hugging and kissing everybody. Elias Martin most of all: the more he would shrink, the more she hugged him. And then, through her jubilation, came the memory of the moments at the beauty shop. She took the stars from her eyes and could see that Elias was terrified. She decided to act. "Elias."

"Yes, Abigail."

"Can we talk?"

"Of course."

She knew it would be a sensitive topic, but it had to be broached. She shuttled him to the other side of the lab, out of eye and earshot of the other researchers, and apologized for having overreacted to her new data; she explained that in her family everybody was very exuberant, and she was sorry she had made him uncomfortable. He mumbled that it wasn't her fault, that everyone made him uncomfortable, especially women, and that she shouldn't worry. As he was explaining, she was stuck by something in his voice, something tender, vulnerable, something she couldn't help but recognize as *hers*. She knew it in a flash, knew it like she knew the atomic weight of cadmium. And so she kissed him, kissed Elias Martin on the lips.

* * *

He tried to resist, but she wouldn't let him. He felt her mouth, felt lips upon his lips for the first time. He felt her breath, her skin against his cheek. This was a woman. He pulled away from her arms, but she held him back, held him to her. In her arms it was like everything that made him afraid; his body was adrift, sliding, liquefying. He was becoming a liquid, he was becoming water, the whole world was water, everything was water, her arms were water, and he was drowning in them. To his eyes, above his eyes, and she kept holding him, kept kissing him, kept drowning him. He was terrified, he was abject, and he was drowning. So he let go. In her arms, beneath the water, the world that had become nothing but water, he just let go. And then she was gone. A finger pressed to his lips, a shush, and she was gone. He heard her in the other side of the lab; she was telling the others to go home, that they would meet for champagne later. He heard the far door clank shut, then open, then clank again. He heard her moving about at her workstation. And then he heard her voice, saying his name. Calling his name as it had never been called before. His feet didn't want to move, they were frozen in the deepwater ice of his fear, and yet he went.

She had cleared off a metal table at the far end of the lab. Two large beakers were filled with the fruit of her successful experiment; they sat in basins of ice water to cool. Abigail Theresa Henderson took the hand of her boss and mentor, led him to the back wall of the lab, turned his back to the table and pressed him up against it. With her other hand, she flicked the light switch, leaving just the light of a single desk lamp to cast its pale glow into the room. And then her hands again, her hands were there on him, holding him, pressing him to her. It was like nothing he had ever felt; it was like the sum of all everythings and he was nothing. Nothing minus nothing, a cipher deliquescing in her arms.

The lips. The hair. She was all hair, hair everywhere, the smell that he couldn't place but knew was her and then realized, yes, shampoo, yes, and it was her. Hair arms lips, he felt himself deeper than drowned, no bubbles, no air. And then her hands were beneath him, and he was sitting on the table, kissing. Kissing a woman. Finally. And then she was sitting next to him and her hands, her hands were taking the arms of his glasses and lifting them off his face. And then he could see nothing, just a mush of color where her face had been, like he was seeing her from underwater. Like he was seeing her from deep underwater.

* * *

She had found her man. When Abigail Henderson had gone to send home her fellow researchers, she had already known that Elias Martin was hers. She also knew she was going to have to do all the work. That was okay; at least there was no ambiguity, and she had read about this many times. She took his glasses from his face with both hands, and though she did it so she could kiss him more easily, she was taken aback by the face she saw. Elias Martin looked handsome. Not studly, not dashing, no

Olivier and certainly no Brando, but in his boyish, befuddled way he looked handsome. To Abigail Henderson he looked more than handsome. His hair was ruffled but thick, his eyes a piercing, if unseeing, green. And he had very, very full, very underused lips.

Once she had his glasses off, she knew she'd get no resistance. She kissed him again even more firmly and pushed him back on the table, climbing on top and straddling him with both legs. She might have liked for her first time if he had taken control, holding her and ravishing her as she had read about, but she knew how shy Elias was, and knew her first time would follow a different storyline.

He had lipstick on his face and clearly couldn't see a thing. So he wasn't prepared when she dragged a finger wet from her tongue down his nose, his lips, his chin, to the top button of his short-sleeved button-down. And there it didn't rest, but flicked, and the button was undone; then the next, and the next, and the one beneath. And then it was off, pens still in the pocket, and the undershirt beneath it. And then Elias Martin felt a sensation that every man knows, that every man feels afresh each time it happens: the exquisite vertigo of being undressed, of looking down and seeing small hands undoing your belt, unzipping your zip. As the belt slipped out of its loops, he too felt the slipping, everything slipping away, so that he might become desire, be lost to desire, and yet he did not stop it.

The belt was open, and tick tick tick tick went the zipper, one tooth at a time. Elias Martin's arms were hanging at his sides like pieces of meat tied to his shoulders. He could not move, he was terrified to move. Abigail Henderson was taking her time, tick

tick tick, while Elias was trying to control the swelling in his pants, trying, pressing his arms down against the table, focusing his mind on not humiliating himself. To no avail, of course, for Abigail Henderson was going to see exactly what she wanted to see.

* * *

There remained the matter of getting her clothes off, of which Elias Martin seemed incapable or unwilling to facilitate. And so Abigail got up off of Elias and stepped back from the table. With trembling fingers she completed the work she had begun: she unlaced Elias Martin's shoes, removed each in turn and the socks as well, pulled his trousers down and off from his ankles, and then began to undress herself as well. Leaving her glasses on, she slipped off her shoes and then her dress, and then slowly, deliberately, took the hand of the sightless Elias Martin and placed it on inch after inch of her exposed flesh. Her neck, her clavicle, the top of her arm. Her wrist, her navel, and then, for the first time since his long-ago infancy, Elias Martin found his hand being placed upon a woman's breast.

Nothing feels like skin. Elias Martin would have become aware of this fact had he been able to notice anything at all above the beating of his heart, the insistence of his erection, and the absolute wonder he felt touching a woman. Before he knew it, before he could make sense of the blobs of color to see what was going on, Abigail had pulled him to his feet, pressed her lips against his, then taken one of the beakers of lubricant from out of its bucket of ice and poured it entire upon the table. The still-warm, ultraslick liquid polyurethane slipped on the surface of the metal table like salmon dropped onto sheerest ice. When she pushed Elias Martin back on it, he could barely stay on, it was so slick. From her purse she took her "always-hopeful" condom (replaced unused every fifteen months), managed at length to rip it open, figured out, on the second try, which direction it unrolled, and with a pinch of her newly invented lubricant, slid it down Elias Martin's virgin cock.

The next thing Abigail Henderson did Elias Martin would have liked to have seen 20/20. With a look of complete determination blended into the beatific face of a woman who has just realized her life's ambition, Abigail Henderson took the other beaker of lubricant in both of her hands and poured it rapturously down her breasts.

* * *

Her body wouldn't have been able to stay on top of his if not for the ballast of his cock inside her. The lubricant between her legs felt fantastic, the lubricant all over them felt fantastic, and Elias Martin between her legs felt fantastic. She moved without knowing how she was moving; she made noises but didn't recognize the sounds coming out of her mouth. Her body pushed forward, forward and down on top of him, pushing then relenting, pushing, pushing. His hands were tight behind her; she couldn't lean back without him pressing her down on top of him again. She felt him inside stretching her, each time as she rocked forward he would go deeper, deeper and ever bigger, like he was inflating inside her with nowhere to go.

He felt himself close to coming, but he couldn't, wouldn't let himself. He would not come, not even with a condom on, not if he could help it. But he felt her on top of him, around him, her weight, her sliding, the squeeze of her pussy, all slick, all tight, him blind, the eye blind, the body blind, fumbling, ridden, bucking, each spasm closer, ever closer, he mustn't, he can't, he mustn't, then closer, another spasm, closer—and then he knew he had no choice.

And Abigail Theresa Henderson, straddled atop Elias Martin, her boss and mentor, let out a scream, a scream of purest pleasure. She screamed because she was wet. She was so very wet. ♦

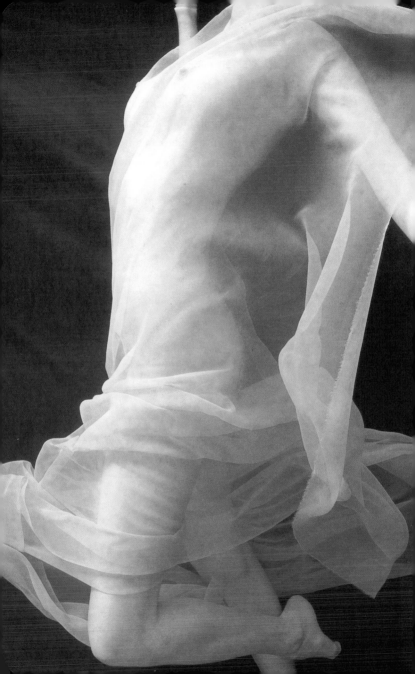

RITE OF SPRING

BY CECILIA TAN

I knew he had the magic in him when I first saw his eyes. How could I not? How could anyone not? Adram Gyrien Hastor, Blood of Tarasco, was reputed to be the first king successor in generations for whom the magic flowed freely. Some, including Arnissa, said it was all talk, all politics to bolster his position. In days of drought, people were hungry and unrest rustled through the countryside like the dried-out stalks of grain in the hot wind. But that day in the courtyard, when he met the daughters for the first time, I stopped doubting.

We, the daughters, were dressed in our finest, despite the mid-day heat. Arnissa was next to me, her gown blue, her lily-white skin and her red hair glowing in the sun bathing the courtyard. My dress was red, my father's colors, of course, my black hair hidden inside the hat they made me wear, to keep my skin—which browned as easily as a chicken's in a fire—out of the sun. The garden was filled with flowers, crisscrossed with flagstones, and

97

I wanted to walk among them and admire them. My own father's gardens had withered to nothing last summer and, with no rain to rejuvenate them this spring, had remained brown and dead. Here in the castle, though, the flowers still grew with careful tending. There was even a healthy stand of the thirstiest of blooms, the delicate blue brookflower. Seeing the tender vine creeping up a stone column was like seeing an old friend, and I wanted to bury my face in the thousand tiny blossoms. But at that moment, we were made to stand still, all twenty of us in a pretty line, as various officials and ministers looked us over before Adram's arrival.

They spoke in whispers, but as my mother used to say, any noblewoman who cannot hear a man's whisper does not deserve her title. My eyes were on the old gardener, making his way from plant to plant with a wooden water bucket and a dipper, ladling out one cup at a time. But I heard when one minister remarked that Adram should be reminded of Arnissa's "favors." He meant the king owed her father a favor, though Arnissa's physical charms were obvious. Mostly they said nothing when they came to me, though I thought one asked if I was too young.

Then we were free to wander the garden, and I used the flowers to shroud my nervousness. I was not too young but was the youngest of the daughters there. Arnissa and my father were close, and she had grown up like an elder sister to me. She, like all the others, was in her twenties. I was not, and I was apprehensive about what was going to happen those weeks we were in the castle. Perhaps if I kept my head down, studying the flowers with my hat shielding my eyes, he'd never notice me.

Many of the flowers were suffering from lack of water despite the gardener's efforts, their petals curled or their leaves drooping. I was standing in a shady corner with Arnissa, lamenting the brookflower's disappearance from my father's land, when Adram was suddenly there in front of us. He had not been announced and was wearing the same plain green tunic and brown boots he wore riding. But I knew it was he all the same, as he approached Arnissa and the serene expression on his face turned to a smile.

Those eyes! As blue as the brookflower with reflections of green in them, but it wasn't their color that startled me. It was their intensity, something in his gaze that made me suck in my breath, and I could see it, sense it, the magic boiling behind those eyes. He had broad shoulders but gentle-looking hands as he took Arnissa's fingers in his own and planted a soft kiss on her knuckles before turning away and moving on down the path.

I could barely speak with my heart suddenly in my throat, but I tried. "Arnissa! Did you see the way he looked at you?"

Arnissa did not match my breathless excitement. She clucked her tongue once. "He's just a man, Melinne."

That was all we said about it then. There were others around and voices carry in a stone courtyard. But I was now sorry that I had gotten my wish. He had walked past me without even a glance, and now my wish was different. I wished desperately that he would turn that gaze on me.

* * *

That night in the women's quarters I sat upon my bed in the room I shared with Arnissa and tried to explain myself.

Arnissa sat at the mirror, the candles all around her, brushing out her hair, which shimmered in the candlelight. Arnissa was, in my opinion, the most beautiful of all the daughters, and given Adram's reaction to her this afternoon, I thought he would choose her, and I told her so.

"And what if he does? In a few weeks it won't matter."

"No, Arnissa, I think you could be the one."

She hissed through her teeth. "Not likely. He'll bed me a few times while he can and then move on."

"Why do you say that?" She sounded so disdainful, and I didn't understand. "You're . . . did you see the way he looked at you today?"

"Like a hungry hunting dog? Of course." She hissed again.

I hugged my knees to my chest, bunching my plain cotton sleeping shift around my ankles. "I think he really liked you."

"He liked my low-cut gown and what was in it."

"But didn't you see the . . . " I wiggled my toes in frustration. "He's going to be king, Arnissa. Doesn't that mean anything to you?"

She put the brush down and turned to face me. "Oh, Melinne, you're still so young. Adram may be the next King of Tarasco, but until he is, he's just another courtier. One who happens to have a privileged opportunity to poke his finger into all of our pies."

I blushed when she said that and hoped the candlelight wouldn't show it. "They say the king successor sometimes just goes with one . . . "

"Not since Meldinor, I believe." She looked almost sad as she leaned toward me and whispered. "Adram's father, they say, put off making his choice until the very last day, and had each of the daughters into his chamber a dozen times."

I shivered a bit at that thought, that a man who was not my husband could have me again and again at will. When we were sent off to the choosing, our mothers invariably said that some of us would never see the successor's bed, and we could return home with our duty fulfilled and our maidenheads intact. Among those he tried, the expectation was that it would be once—one night for the sake of the country, the strength of the kingship, and the health of the nation. And no man could turn away a woman who had been blessed with the king's seed. His own sons would grow up strong as a result, his animals and crops, too . . . which raised a question in my mind.

"You mean, King Hastor bedded" —here I blushed again— "them all?"

"Multiple times."

"But then, why weren't there more children?"

Arnissa wrinkled her nose. "Because the magic in Hastor's blood is thin. And I expect his son is going to be the same."

I shook my head—I wanted to argue. I was sure Adram was different. But I didn't know what to say or how to explain it.

We both jumped at the knock on the door. A moment later it opened, and an old man in a white robe stuck his head in. He was blind but not mute, and he called out Arnissa's name. We exchanged glances. So it was the first night, and Arnissa had already been chosen. As she took the arm of the blind old man, he led her along the corridor with one hand on a golden rope that threaded along one wall. I stood in the hallway watching him lead her to the end, where they turned and disappeared out of sight.

I lay down on the bed and knew that I should sleep. But I could not. I let the candles burn low and sputter out one by one, but no darkness came behind my eyes as I lay there trying to imagine what was occurring in the sacred chambers. Would she lie down upon the bed, looking up at him? I pictured her lying back upon the platform. He would kneel at her feet and say a brief prayer before pushing her shift up to her belly and spreading her knees apart. He would lie between her legs then, moving himself up and down until he found the right place, and then he would be inside her. She would have the Blood of Tarasco inside her and she would be blessed.

I rolled over and was surprised by the wetness between my own legs. I could feel the slipperiness in my crotch, and I squeezed my legs together. I bunched my shift between my knees, pulled up my blanket, and tried to sleep, with the vision of Adram's eyes still burning in my head.

Sometime later I was woken by the sound of the door opening. Moonlight came through our window and I knew some hours must have passed. Arnissa came in, and the attendant closed the door behind her. She sat down on her bed.

I sat up and stared at her. Her hair was more disheveled than before and she made no move to brush it out before lying down. She lay back upon her pillow like she was very tired.

"Well?" I squeaked.

Arnissa gave a quiet laugh. "It was what it was, Melinne. Nothing to be afraid of."

"Aren't you going to tell me about it?"

"What is there to tell? His thorn pricked my rose." Her words were tough, but I could tell by her voice that she was not. She was crying very softly.

"But don't you feel blessed? Didn't you feel . . . "

"The magic? Please, Melinne," she said, her voice growing harsh. "Grow up. Magic is for children's stories. If my husband thinks I'm going to bring him something special because the king-to-be plowed the furrow before him, then all the more fool him."

Her crying was making me cry, too, as it always did. "Was it . . ." I didn't understand what could have made her so upset. "Did it hurt?"

She came over to my bed and hugged me. "Oh, poor little Melinne. Don't be afraid. No, it didn't hurt. He was very gentle. I'm just tired is all." She kissed me on the forehead and then climbed back into her bed. "Have a good night, now."

She still thought I was afraid of him, and maybe I was in a way, but with her words ringing in my ears I wanted even more to be chosen. *He was very gentle. . . .*

* * *

But time went on and I was not chosen. I thought Arnissa would be the one, though. She went again and again to Adram's chamber, until she no longer cried when she came back to our room. She would just climb into bed and go to sleep, or pretend to, and I gave up trying to ask her about what had happened.

But there was gossip and talk among the daughters, as we would sit to do needlework in the afternoons or as we would eat.

Soon I began to feel I was the only one Adram had not taken to his bed, and when the attendant would come for Arnissa, my heart would leap, hoping that this time it would be me, and after she would leave, it would be me that lay in bed and cried.

We would see Adram every few days, either all eating together in the grand hall, him seated to his father's right at the table above ours, or in the gardens. He shone, his hair brown and straight and gleaming, cut short for a helm, and those eyes, always those eyes. I had never felt this way about a boy or man before, and felt helpless to slake the thirst he brought out in me. I wished I had a way to catch the attention of those eyes and more than once almost reached out to touch his sleeve. But I did not.

In our room one night, Arnissa returned and, as soon as the door closed, flung herself down on the bed.

"What's wrong?" I asked, sitting up.

"He's a pig," she answered, "just like his father."

"I . . . I thought you said he was gentle. . . ."

"I told you before, Melinne. He just wants to poke his finger into all of our pies, that's all."

I sighed. I wanted to tell her how much I wished it was me he called. I almost told her again of what I saw in his eyes that very first day, but it was as if I could already hear her voice replying to me. She would tell me I was just a silly girl, too young to really know, young enough to fall for a handsome face. "If you dislike it so much, why does he keep asking for you?"

Arnissa sat up and stared at me in the light of the sputtering candles I had let burn down, as always. "Melinne, I don't let him know I don't like it."

"Why?"

She shook her head. "There's just no explaining anything to you, is there." She sighed. "I shouldn't seem as if I'm ungrateful for the so-called blessing, should I? I mustn't make trouble for my father at court, isn't that right?"

"Yes, yes, I suppose. . . . "

"So no one knows how much I hate being taken to Adram's bedchamber, except you." She lay back and seemed disinclined to talk any further.

But what she did not know was that I had let it slip to one of the other daughters already, a few days before. Some of them, I knew, wanted very much to be queen, but did not seem to be enjoying the act itself. Others wanted to go back to the lives that they knew, but they were not unhappy about Adram's attentions. Surely, I thought, there were others like Arnissa who wanted neither the queenship nor his attentions? What was the harm in admitting that to one another? But as I lay there I went through the list of daughters in my head, thinking of the whispers I had exchanged with each of them over the weeks that had passed . . . it seemed upon my tally that Arnissa was the only one who wanted nothing to do with Adram at all. I was ashamed then of what I had done: whenever the women put their heads together to whisper, I had talked about Arnissa and not about myself. They would have pitied me, or poked fun at me, the runt of the litter who dreamed of being queen, that's the way they would have seen it. But I could not have cared less about the throne. All I wanted was for him to look into my eyes, to touch me, for our lips to meet. That was not something I could say to the other daughters, so I kept my feelings hidden, and had ransomed Arnissa's feelings in their place. I knew then that trouble was coming.

* * *

It arrived the next day when a cleric, one of the Keepers of the Magic, addressed the daughters as we were gathered together in a windowless meeting chamber deep in the center of the castle. It seemed an odd place for us, quite different from the usual audience chamber, but when we heard what he had to say, I realized why we were there. "It has come to our attention," he said, his deep blue robes making him almost invisible in the ill-lit room, "that one of you is reluctant to perform her duties." Like the court-trained ladies that we were, we sat straight and did not look around at one another. That room was cut off from other areas of the castle, impossible to eavesdrop on, and the only place for such an admission to be made aloud. The cleric droned on, then, telling us again what we had heard so many times, that in order for the magic to manifest we had to believe in it, we had to surrender ourselves to it. We were half of what was needed, the rain that makes the seed blossom, and so on. For some reason, listening to him tell the tale then, it sounded less convincing than when my own father had explained it to me. Perhaps it was the tone of his voice, almost mocking us, as if he himself did not believe a word of it.

When he came to the end of his speech, though, we all sat up to take notice. "We know which one of you it is. She will be called tonight. If her resistance is not broken, then the choosing will fail, so it is of tantamount importance that she surrender herself utterly to our king successor." He went on, about how the drought would worsen, the cattle would fall ill, and so on, if the choosing failed, but I was barely listening. My heart beat hard in my chest and I wanted so much to look up at Arnissa, but I could not.

Instead I looked around the room again. The torches had been hastily lit when we had first entered, but they were burning steadily now and I could see into the corners where, before, my sun-dazzled eyes could not. There were chains on the walls.

"Her resistance will be broken," the cleric said with finality, as if this were one thing he truly had faith in.

* * *

It was a long, long day. After the speech they pretended as if nothing had happened, and we ate, practiced our dancing, and did our needlework just as we did on any other day. So it was not until that night that I finally had a moment alone with Arnissa.

I immediately told her it was my fault that they knew. "I'm so sorry, Arnissa! I never dreamed . . ."

"Hush, it's done with now." Her hair shimmered like flames in the candlelight.

"But they're going to do something horrible to you, I know it."

She sat on her bed in her white shift, shaking her head slowly. A few tears fell into her lap. "There's nothing you can do, Melinne."

Just then the knock came at the door, and suddenly I knew what to do. "Yes, there is," I told her.

Before she could argue, I took the arm of the blind attendant and it was me he led out of the room.

The castle was large and full of twisting stairways and corridors, and yet the blind man knew his way around them, his hand upon the ropes. We went through areas where there were no torches at all, and I had to cling to his arm to keep from stumbling. But of course, I realized—a blind man needs no torches. They did not want the daughters to know where Adram's chamber was, so that we could not visit him unannounced and thereby influence his decision. As we stepped through the pitch blackness, though, I sensed we were heading back to the room where the cleric had spoken to us that day.

My heart was beating hard and felt like it was trying to climb up out of my throat. So at last I was taking the walk to Adram's chamber that I had dreamed of every night since coming to the castle, but this time it would not be to his bed. What was I thinking?

We reached the door of the chamber and I walked in of my own accord. The cleric was there with his back to me, and I was unsure what to do. Adram was nowhere in sight. My plan had been to tell Adram that I had lied, that when I had said Arnissa had not wanted to go, I had been talking about myself and trying to deflect the blame. But faced with the dour cleric, I found I could not say anything at all.

He turned to face me and frowned as he looked me up and down. "So, you are the one? Come here."

I stepped forward and he seemed to get taller with each step I took. He then pulled a hood over my head and I could see nothing more. Behind me he tightened the hood so that it was snug against my eyes, covering my hair, my ears, my nose, but leaving my mouth and chin free so I could breathe. He led me over to the wall and pushed my back against it. I heard the clank of chain and then he wrapped my wrists in leather that creaked like a horse's saddle as he lifted my arms up over my head. I guessed that he had attached the leather to a metal ring set in the wall. I was trembling. This was not the night as I had imagined it, with the gentle, loving Adram planting his seed in me while we gazed into each other's eyes.

The hood covered my ears but I could still hear. Someone else came into the room, the door closed heavily behind him, and I heard Adram's voice. "Is all in readiness?"

"Yes, your highness," the cleric answered. "I have brought the book in case you would like me to refer to it."

"Do you think that will be necessary?"

"With all respect, your highness, you have no experience in breaking the will of a human being and may need some advice."

"And what would you advise me to do now?"

"You must assert yourself over her, prove to her that she is utterly and completely within your control. Remember, it is sur- render we are seeking, ultimately. She must feel as though she has not a shred of her own will left." The cleric cleared his throat. "You could begin by tearing her clothes off."

I heard Adram's boots on the stone as he approached me. How could I not feel as if I was utterly and completely within his control? I was chained to a wall, helpless. I felt his hands take hold of the cloth around my neck and then his muscles strain, his breath warm on my lips for a moment before the seam gave way and tore down the middle. He jerked the cloth a few more times and then the shift was rent all the way to my feet.

I felt his hand caress my chin and I shivered. He leaned close and I was expecting a kiss, but then I heard the cleric's voice. "A slap would do better than that, my lord."

Adram hissed. "Not on her face."

"You are supposed to be showing her no respect, my lord."

"Not on her face, Keeper," he repeated.

"Then turn her."

I felt his hands on me then, as he turned me under the ring so that my face was to the stone. I felt then the edge of a blade against my neck as he slipped his knife into my sleeve and swiftly cut the rest of the shift away. Now I was naked against the stone and I felt one of his hands on my shoulder. His other hand slid down my back and between my buttocks. I sucked in my breath. How many times had I lain in bed, dreaming about him doing just that? One finger insinuated itself into the slippery folds, and I could not help but push back into him.

"Keeper, she is wet."

"And of what concern is that to us, your highness?"

Adram's voice crackled with suppressed anger. I felt I could almost see his face through the hood. "Does that not indicate that her body is ready for me?"

"Perhaps, but it is her body only, my lord."

His hand drew back then, and through the hand that was still on my shoulder I felt him tense as he drew back for the blow. His hand fell upon my bare buttocks with a loud smack and I cried out. At what point, I wondered, would the Keeper decide it was enough, and allow Adram to plant his seed? I held the leather between my hands and squeezed it hard as the next blow came. And the next, and the next. Sometimes I was able to hold back my cry, but mostly I was not. I counted ten, then twenty, and then I lost count, gritting my teeth and wailing and waiting for it to be over.

And then came Adram's hand, soothing the sore skin. I trembled hard, sobbing against the stone. Such a gentle touch! I craved it again and pressed back into him. I could feel the rough cloth of his tunic against my skin, and the bone of his hip. No, not his hip. I sucked in a breath as I realized what I was rubbing against. Adram was eager for me, and his finger again slid down into the cleft between my legs. I was dripping with honey, now.

"Keeper, she is ready. She's never done that before."

"You know perfectly well, your highness, that a wild horse may feign tameness."

Adram hissed, but softly. "And what does your book suggest we do next?"

I heard the leaves of a book being turned. "Why, your highness, we've barely begun."

Adram left me then, and I surmised he was looking at the book as well.

The cleric's voice continued. "We have all of these means at your disposal. Whips, flails, needles, candles, braided rope. . . ."

The next thing I heard I can describe only as a growl, and then the sound of the book hitting the floor. "I'll not ruin her and I'll not perform for you like a trained animal."

"Your highness . . . "

"Your title may be Keeper, but who is it who holds the power here?"

"My lord, I meant only . . . " Then all was silent for a few moments, and I heard the cleric gasp. "My lord, your eyes . . .!"

Adram's voice was soft again. "Are you surprised?"

"I, I . . . " the cleric stammered into a silent wonder.

"Did you think the power would not manifest in me?" I heard Adram's boots as he walked back and forth. "Did you not believe?"

"I never dared to hope that . . . " The cleric cleared his throat and tried to reassert himself. "Clearly the ritual has worked. She must be ready to give herself to you or . . . "

Adram's voice sounded like he could barely contain himself. "I am not like my father. My blood is not so thin. Now, go."

I heard the rustle of cloth and then the door opened and shut.

And then Adram's hands were running down my back. I tingled everywhere he touched and I moaned out loud. He turned me again, so that my back was to the stone and my lips could meet his. We chewed hungrily at each other's mouths, and I thought I would almost cry for joy. His body pressed against mine, the roughness of his clothes against my bare skin, the hardness of him pressing into the softness of me. I wrapped my legs around him and pulled him in tight.

"Slowly, slowly," he admonished.

I thrashed and tried to squeeze him harder with my legs.

He chuckled. "I suppose it is a blessing that you are tied there." He caressed my cheek. "I know, I feel it, too. But do you know what would happen if I were to plunge into you this instant, my dear?"

"What?" I whispered back.

"All the power we feel, all the magic we've gathered, you and I, would dissipate in an instant. And we haven't gathered nearly enough." Adram brushed his lips past mine. "The Keepers know only what is in their books. I know what is in a king's heart."

I felt him pull back then. "Don't go!"

"Do not fear, my sweet, I am right here." And then I could hear the sounds of him disrobing. "Much as I prefer my own chambers for this, perhaps the Keepers were right about this one thing. I have never felt such a surge of the power."

The next thing I felt was his fingers along my ribs, and then his tongue wrapped itself around one of my nipples, and the tingling I felt in my body grew. He lapped at the other then, as his fingers cupped the mound of my crotch, one finger making its slow way toward the center like the blind man to the dungeon. I let out another cry as he slid it back and forth, and shook my arms, trying to free myself so I could hold him, pull him to me.

"Calmly, calmly, my sweet," he whispered, as his sliding finger moved faster in the wetness there, and I thought perhaps I would faint from the hard beating of my heart and the feeling surging through me. Then he slowed and I could breathe again.

"Please," I managed to choke out, once my breathing slowed. "Please, Adram, let me see your eyes."

He pressed himself against me then, his chest to my chest, his lips to my lips, and reached behind me to fumble with the ties of the hood. It came loose, and I felt my hair slide down my neck, even as his hands slid it from me. He cupped my face in his hands then as we kissed. I opened my eyes first, in time to see him open his.

It was not my imagination. His eyes glowed. Then they widened in surprise. "Melinne, daughter of Gilliman?"

"Yes, your highness." I could not get my voice above a whisper.

"But how could you be the one who . . . ?"

I put one of my legs around one of his and pulled him closer. "As you have seen, the Keepers are not right about everything."

He kissed me again then, letting the kiss move southward, over my neck and down to the hollow between my breasts. His hands followed his mouth, and he caressed my nipples with his thumbs, making me cry out again. "Adram . . ." I said, unable to say anything more. "Adram . . . "

When he came up for air he said, "Can you see your reflection in my eyes?"

I shook my head. The candles and torches were not strong enough, and the inner light in his eyes burned brightly.

"Your eyes burn like mine," he said into my ear. "You are the one."

"Adram, please. . . . " What could I say? "Please, I don't think I can wait any longer."

He looked at the straps of leather above my head. "When the time is right, my sweet." But he began parting my legs with his, and I felt the hard length of him against my mound. With one hand, he swept it back and forth in the wetness, and I whimpered. Then he put one of his hands under one of my buttocks, and lifted me a few inches, just enough so that the head of him slid between my legs into the wetness. He slicked it well and then pressed me into the wall, his thorn only then settling against the center of my rose.

He came into me an inch at a time, and my legs shook and I cried out as every part of me wanted him at that moment. He crept in, and then backed himself slowly out. He repeated it with excruciating slowness, again and again. But when I looked up into his eyes, I saw that they burned brighter than ever. He was trembling also now, sweat beading on his forehead as he struggled to hold himself back.

And then he began to increase his pace, bit by bit. He had both hands planted on my buttocks and pulled me onto him with increasing speed. Energy was pouring into me then, and I strained toward him. I heard a snap then and my arms came free—I had broken the leather strap and we tumbled to the floor, but did not separate. Now I hooked my legs behind his, and held him to me with my arms, and he drove me into the floor with the force of his thrusts. The energy just built and built and built until, as they describe it in the legends, we were both consumed by it. We were both screaming as we hit the release point, clinging to each other as the dam burst. I felt as though I could see across the country, a cow giving birth in one of my father's paddocks, a wolf mounting his mate, Arnissa's sister Hellenne suckling her firstborn son. The magic raced out from us to everywhere in the kingdom.

Arnissa told me later that a thundercloud had gathered that night, its rumblings growing louder and louder until the whole castle was suddenly shaken by a tremendous clap, and then it had begun to rain. As the storm moved across the country, people ran out of their houses and danced in the streets of the villages. Down in the dungeon we heard none of it, but the next day the brookflower in the garden had grown as high as the second story. The daughters wove countless blossoms into my hair for the bonding ceremony, and when my father's retinue arrived, there were petals aplenty strewn in his path, for he was now the father of a queen. ◆

GISELLE

BY LOREN MACLEOD

I am a respectable woman, not in the habit of soliciting men for money, but I am also poor and find myself suddenly faced with the staggering cost of drainage, which is sure to be at least one thousand francs. There is an ornamental lake at the bottom of the inner courtyard of the *palais* and, alas, its level is rising quickly. This morning, after opening the French doors to the balcony, I watched with dismay as the water lapped through the wrought-iron railing and over the terra-cotta tiles. The balconies off the other ground-floor apartments are also partially submerged. If only they were still occupied, so that I could take up a collection among my fellow tenants to pay the drainage bill! The lake will soon flood the apartments themselves. *Alors,* it must be at least ten feet deep by now.

Deep enough, I see, to attract a shark.

L'Ancienne Cité is sinking. It is slowly, but inexorably, being deluged by the water released by the melting of the North and South Poles. L'Ancienne (as the old city is known informally) was built many centuries ago over a network of canals fed by the river Seine, and these ornamental lakes are connected to the canals via ancient tunnels our erstwhile municipal government has promised but, in most cases, failed to seal. I blame the government for the flooding and for the presence of the shark, which swam through the tunnel and devoured all of the pretty goldfish that inhabited the lake when it was a much shallower affair. I enjoyed standing on the balcony and tossing bread crumbs to these fish, and a terrible unease blooms in my heart as I watch the shark circle around and around within the foursquare confines of the courtyard, hunting for new victims.

It is not yet half past eight o'clock, but already crowds of men are hurrying through the arcaded plaza on their way to the cratered steps of the Grand Canal, where boats wait to ferry them across the Seine to their offices in *La Nouvelle Cité*. With my paying houseguest, Solange, away at her morning classes, I can do as I wish with the apartment and my body. I am petite, fine-boned, and have small, smooth-skinned features. It is therefore easy for me to pass as a schoolgirl. I know from observing neighborhood goings-on that the most successful prostitutes often do. So, after nibbling at a baguette to calm my stomach, I put on a short woolen skirt and a pale blue blouse with a prim white collar of the Peter Pan variety. I remove my underpants. My feet slip into heavy brown shoes. There is the final matter of braiding my hair into two pigtails, and then I find myself loitering awkwardly in the shadows of the western doorway of the *palais* (the eastern doorway faces the Canal de Louis XIX and is approachable only by boat).

I wait for a likely candidate with a bubble in my throat. I feel humiliated and frightened but do not have much of a choice; there is less and less money to be made translating Italian books into French, which is my only source of income. If it were not for Solange I should be unable to pay the rent and buy food for the *garde-manger.* But the drainage must occur, and my landlord has taken the scoundrel's way out by claiming financial difficulties due to the outflux of hydrophobic tenants from this, the least profitable of his numerous real-estate holdings (a claim I do not have the resources to contest before a judge). The landlord cares not a whit that I—and thousands of others—will become homeless when L'Ancienne finally succumbs to the rising waters. I have no family, no friends, no savings account. Only a string of old amours who would be hard pressed to lend me the occasional *sou,* let alone one thousand francs.

Jean was the only pearl on that string, and we shared a sweat-soaked love that still causes me to awaken in the middle of the night, gasping and entangled in the bed linen.

Nobody notices me. The crowds disturb flocks of pigeons, which fly up to roost on the spires of the crumbling basilica across the plaza, which can flood to the depth of a foot in rainy weather. Most of these men are low-level office workers and shop assistants who cannot afford to live across the river in La Nouvelle but find houses in the suburbs equally dear. I look up. The sky, as usual, is as blank as an ironed sheet. I look back down—aha!—here comes a short, gray-haired man in a good suit. He walks slowly, observing everything and everyone around him. I catch his eye and hastily unbutton my blouse to show him what is there. Nothing much, but he nods and smiles. His teeth seem to be composed largely of incisors. Since I am not a professional (not established in this trade like the girl-women who haunt the side-streets of L'Ancienne and maintain covert arrangements with the proprietors of questionable hotels), I usher him silently into the *palais* itself, which was the summer residence of a Russian countess who lived seven hundred years ago. Its galleries and reception rooms are now subdivided into dozens of apartments and depressing little suites. Plaster flakes from the vaulted ceilings. Stinking canal water overflows the cellar to form puddles on the marble floors.

At my client's request I give a brief tour of the apartment. "Some trouble for you, miss," he says, and points down at the slimy green moss that has sprouted between the submerged tiles of the balcony. There is a disconcerting opacity in his eyes, which are a gray paler than his hair. I would like to conclude the session as soon as possible: "Here is a better view, sir." My second successful attempt at coquettishness. We slip into my bedroom and quickly disrobe. What a loathsome body he has, fat and white and slack. The shark, in contrast, is taut-skinned and lithe. I shudder at the reality of both of them as I obey his slap-accompanied order to press my breasts into his groin. My mind darts about frantically, desperate for distraction, and finds shelter in a memory of Jean, who has lured me to a bed in a cheap hotel and bent me over a mound of pillows, the better to spread the halves of my bottom and insert his rough, impossibly wet tongue into the plumping folds of my vagina. At the same time he runs his long, callused fingers up and down my inner thighs, each caress exactly matching the advance and retreat of his tongue as I moan and knead the threadbare counterpane, digging my heels into his armpits and trying to open more of myself to him. It seems amazing, but he has reached so far with that serpentine tongue as to lick the closed threshold of my cervix, which he teases, teases, teases until the ring of muscle relaxes and allows him into even that innermost chamber, and I cry out—

"Unh-unh! *Sacre bleu!*"

My legs are hooked over my client's fleshy shoulders when he comes with a gush of fluid that smells faintly of sewage. The session nets me his name (Guy) and, because I am an unassertive novice, a mere forty francs. However, he offers to pay me double next time if I "agree" to experience *la petite morte*—orgasm—with him. This future rendezvous will take place at his office, he says, so that his wife will not eventually find out about his activities from the local busybodies she calls friends. After he goes I drink a glass of wine and watch the shark play in the lake. It uses its eight fins to roll itself over and over in the water like a trained porpoise. What a repulsively fascinating spectacle. This species feeds on whatever is thrown or swept into the canals from kitchen windows and marketplace squares: spoiled vegetables, rotten fruit, fish entrails, even the contents of chamber pots. They are also albino from millennia of dwelling in the pitch-black muck at the bottom of the Seine (they rise to the surface only if baited with raw meat). I suspect that this one likes the fact that the *palais* is extraordinarily tall—five stories instead of the usual two or three—so sunlight never penetrates the inky water. The shark is also, I think, hoping for the miraculous appearance of more goldfish.

I really don't know what upsets me more: the shark, or the sight of my shame-filled face in the tarnished mirrors set into the walls of the kitchen, which was carved out of a gilded salon where aristocrats used to dance the *quadrille* and intellectuals argued philosophy over games of whist. To distract myself from these unhappy reflections, I take a knife and draw many short lines of blood in the unblemished skin of my inner forearm. I bind the wounds with a strip of cloth torn from the sheet on which I consorted with Guy, and then cook lunch for Solange and myself. She always comes home at one.

Nothing makes Solange happier than a steaming platter of spaghetti and a big bowl of salad. She is very young, pretty, and easy to please. She waves her fork around as she expounds breezily upon Balzac and Racine. She has no financial worries; her parents send her a check for two hundred francs each month for her school and living expenses. They are appalled, of course, that she has chosen to live "squalidly" in the doomed environs of L'Ancienne, and with an infrequently employed translator, to boot.

"What about the balcony, eh? It is a disaster."

I am very patient with Solange. "I will find some manner of paying the cost of drainage, and then I will threaten the government with a lawsuit unless it agrees to block the tunnel."

"Giselle! What has happened to your arm?"

"Nothing. A burn from the pot, that is all."

"Take off that ridiculous piece of cloth. I shall make a poultice for it, and a proper bandage."

"No, Solange. It is nothing, I swear."

"Are you certain?"

"I am certain."

"What a peculiar costume you are wearing today. Is it new?"

That night I awake from a terrible dream in which I find myself wallowing in the thick layer of sewage at the bottom of a canal. Feeling and eating excrement. Hoping to encounter the sunken carcass of a chicken. For hours afterward I pace the checkerboard tiles in the hall, listening to Solange's contented snores and smoking imported American cigarettes I cannot really afford to buy. I think about Guy and about Jean, who is far away in Deauville with his new woman. I grind each cigarette out on the soft skin of my inner thighs until daybreak pinks the sky over the city, and I am finally able to doze off on a velvet ottoman I rescued years ago from the cellar. When I wake up again I find a fresh pot of *café-filtre* on the stove, and a note from Solange saying she has gone to class and is sorry I didn't sleep well.

Guy expects me at noon, at the start of his lunch hour. I bathe, dress up as a schoolgirl again, put on a light summer jacket, and hire a boat to take me across the foaming gray waters of the Seine. La Nouvelle was founded on the heights of a granite palisade and boasts hundreds of modern high-rise buildings made of glass and steel and concrete that feature atriums and dry-floored airshafts in place of ornamental lakes. Guy's law firm, the one he clerks for, is located in one of these atrocities. When I disembark, I am knocked to the ground by a throng of hungry, stern-faced men headed for cafés and restaurants. My throat constricts from the acrid fumes of automobiles, which are forbidden in L'Ancienne due to its narrow streets and unstable bridges. There is too much noise here, too: screeching tires, honking horns, shouted curses. By the time I reach my destination I am in tears and, I daresay, would be unable to pursue *la petite morte* with even the gorgeous film actor Yves Delon, let alone Guy.

"Madame Merteuil!"

Guy's Internet-addicted colleagues glance up irritably at me from their computer screens. He introduces me via this false name as the wife of an important client of the firm and ushers me hastily into the handsomely appointed office of one of the senior partners, who is in London for a conference. I think this is outrageously daring, and tell him so. He orders me to pull up my skirt and bend naked over the desk while he stands behind me, unbuttoning his trousers. This position reveals the cigarette burns, but Guy merely grunts with approval. Propped up on my elbows, I stare down at my reflection in the polished mahogany expanse of the desk and . . .

Jean's sun-bronzed face appears over my shoulder; he is moving his tall, lithe-muscled body over and onto my back. His skin is as slick as wet satin. I feel his heart beating through his ribs. He cups my breasts in his enormous, work-worn hands and pinches the nipples too hard, the way I like, and I whimper. The edge of the desk jams against my hipbones, forced against the wood by his powerful thighs. The length of his penis is thicker and harder than a pipe, and is pressed deep into the heated crevice of my bottom. One of his fingers finds and rubs the button of my clitoris. Then, suddenly, his face disappears for a terrible moment in which I think I have lost him forever. I grovel, I whine obscenities. I entreat God for various sexual favors. I reach behind me and part my buttocks with my hands, begging like a wretch until, mercifully, there is the masterful prod of his cock against my anus.

He eases it in, inch by precious inch. I gasp. I weep disconsolately. I give a part of myself up with each mighty thrust. My swollen breasts jerk back and forth over the cold surface of the desk. I absorb Jean's passion with the cushioned vertebrae of my spinal column. It is an impersonal, relentless battering, and I succumb to its sweet power in shudders that rack us both.

The reverie dissolves with Guy's abrupt withdrawal from my vagina. I am still bent over the desk. His strange-smelling fluid drips down my thighs and stings the burns. When I stand up and turn around I am surprised and alarmed to find him flushed with rage. "*Jean* is not my name!" Before I can react, Guy grabs and rips out the front of my blouse, baring my breasts. He lunges forward and fastens his lips on my left nipple and nearly bites it off in an ecstasy of hatred. I scream and throw myself away from him, clasping my jacket to my bosom. When I look back at him on my panicked way out, I am met by only the mad, silvery glitter in his eyes. And his mouth, stretched with crazed laughter, the teeth stained pink with my blood.

"Did I say forty francs?" he shrieks. "I meant eighty!"

And then: *"One thousand francs, Giselle."*

When Solange comes home for lunch she finds me unconscious on the kitchen floor and revives me with smelling salts and begs me to tell her what is wrong. She is shocked by what she hears, but even more shocked by the wounds on my breast and thighs. As I babble out the entire sordid story, I feel miserable, miserable, and horribly ashamed. I am not worth the price of the blanket she drapes around my shoulders, not deserving of the hot tea she prepares and presses to my lips.

"I don't understand. I never loved him. I never told him my name."

"So?"

"Do you know, Solange, that I believe Guy may be the shark."

Solange shakes her head emphatically, and her sumptuous, brown-nippled breasts sway back and forth under the semi-transparent confines of her muslin camisole. "You are hysterical, *chérie,* and need a good rest. In the country, yes? Fresh air and cows. My aunt owns a cottage in Deauville. It has not been occupied for some time, and I have a copy of the key. I will pack our things after my final exam tomorrow and we will go there on the train."

"But what will happen to our apartment? Solange, L'Ancienne is sinking. Our *palais* is sinking! Soon only the upper floors will be visible above the water."

She places her hand over mine. It is the first time she has touched me with tenderness, and electricity thrums through the center of my bones. My eyes are still fastened on her camisole. An unbidden scene flashes across my mind: I am sucking each fat-nippled breast, paying homage to each one in turn, while Solange arches her back and cups the back of my head with her hand to bring my mouth even closer to her flesh.

"Then together we shall watch L'Ancienne sink. From the deck of a tour boat, if you like. We shall toast its great age and beauty with a bottle of champagne and lament its destruction at the hands of man."

"Do you know, Solange, that he offered to pay me double if I had an orgasm?"

"What is that?"

In the morning, after Solange has gone to sit her exam, I open the French doors, step down barefoot onto the flooded balcony, and climb over the railing. There is a moment of hesitation before I launch myself into the lake. The icy water shocks my body; it is like bathing in chilled ink. I tread water for a little while, then hold my breath and duck my head below the surface, peering avidly into the shadows. The shark appears at once—a pale, undulating shape reminiscent of a tapeworm. I continue to tread water in the corner closest to the balcony, keeping my arms outstretched protectively before me. The shark approaches. Swims closer and closer. A smile suddenly appears in its rubbery, unbroken skin to reveal a hinged jaw and a throat lined with rows and rows of sharp teeth. When it darts forward, I use my hands to grab it by the pectoral fins and clasp it to my bosom. Once in my embrace the shark becomes surprisingly delicate, the bones as fine and cartilaginous as those of a sardine, and I do not hesitate to snap its spine.

This species, you see, is unusually small—no more than three or four times the length of a goldfish. It was only my fear that made it seem so much larger than it really was. ◆

SEAFOOD COCKTAIL

BY CONNIE WILKINS

He emerged from the sea like the incarnation of some primal god, wet, powerful, gleaming as darkly as polished rosewood. When he spoke, his voice was deep as thunder, smooth as rain.

"Hey, Lexie, where do you think they've hidden the cameras?"

I rolled out from under the boat's inverted hull. In spite of the jagged hole in its prow, it had provided some refuge during last night's tempest. "Come on, Max, you think they could fake a storm like that? Even if the technology existed, they wouldn't pay for it. The beauty of reality shows is the low overhead."

"You're probably right," he admitted, turning away to block a full frontal view. His shyness seemed contradictory for someone who'd signed away all rights to privacy for a chance at fame and fortune.

I still got the benefit of his muscular butt. Droplets of seawater trickled over its curves, forming jaunty question marks. Several intriguing answers occurred to me.

"You'd think they'd still cover all the bases," he said over his shoulder. "Including any island we might get ourselves shipwrecked on. Otherwise, why let us have a boat, even a chickenshit one like that?"

He might have a point there. Besides the one he was keeping out of view. "I just hope they know this sand spit exists," I said. "We could've been blown a hundred miles or more from the main island." I peeled off my sodden T-shirt and shorts and spread them next to his on the hull to dry. The fact that I was naked now, too, didn't seem to put him at ease. "You can search for cameras all you like—I'll even help after I wash this sand off," I added. "But I think our first priority should be figuring out how to survive until they come to get us."

I walked into the whispering wavelets of the lagoon, feeling his eyes on me, and feeling my body move in ways subtly different from the strides I would have taken under the gaze of another woman. A tingle spread across my buttocks and around to my belly and upward to my breasts; it had been a long time since a masculine presence had had that effect.

I swam out until the water was smooth enough for me to float on my back, letting the tension of last night's ordeal dissolve. The sudden, chaotic storm; the hours of clinging to the capsized boat; the grinding impact against the reef; images flowed together, coiled into and out of each other, like oil on the surface of a whirlpool. The one clear memory was a sexual current intensified by fear. Max and I had huddled close through the night under our meager shelter, our bodies pressed so tightly together that our clothes, saturated with rain and sweat and seawater, were no barrier to the pounding of each other's heart. But Max, in spite of the arousal his wet jeans did little to conceal, had done nothing to take it any farther.

I had a pretty good idea why. He had witnessed my girlfriend Tonya's explicitly steamy farewell at the plane and drawn the obvious conclusion. But Tonya had known perfectly well that potential sex was written between the lines of the show's contract, and she'd still pressured me to sign it. I'd agreed to do the Marooned show, with a dozen people dumped on an island and left without supplies, cell phones, or even a crew to man the supposedly hidden cameras, only for my indie-producer girlfriend's sake. If I could get a bit of notoriety, she figured, she'd have a better chance of getting backers for the films she wanted to make with me.

But all of that had seemed distant and unreal while the rain pounded around us, making our shelter into an impenetrable cave. Max's arms around me and mine around him had seemed absolutely right for that isolated moment, and the lightning flashes outside had built an electric tension deep inside me until I'd been at the point of jumping him myself when he'd started snoring softly.

Men! But he'd saved my life more than once in the last few hours, maybe even a time or two more than I'd saved his. Instead of interrupting his exhausted sleep, I'd amused myself with working my hand gently, gently between jeans and skin and teasing his heavy balls and straining cock just lightly enough to make him writhe and groan in his dreams, until, ultimately, his pants were soaked with something thicker and sweeter than seawater. And all without waking up.

I drifted onward in the lagoon, savoring a gentler tension. Unless Max had more reason for resistance than figuring me for a hard-core dyke, being marooned was going to get very interesting, very soon. My stomach had been rumbling in hunger for at least a week, but now I had a growing appetite for a type of meat I hadn't tasted for a long, long time. I swung upright, my toes just touching the sandy bottom.

Max was still on shore, dragging the boat up toward the sparse shade of a few palm trees. I looked around and saw I'd drifted close to a rocky outcropping that formed a tiny islet near the center of the lagoon.

The urge to explore was countered by caution. A maze of underwater rocks surrounded the islet, suggesting mysterious, lurking creatures, maybe octopi. I could see, too close to pass up, clusters of what I was pretty sure were oysters. I wished I had pockets, to carry some back; my built-in pockets winced at the thought of rough oyster shells. I dived and grasped a large one in each hand. Later Max and I could check out the area together. First, though, I had an urge for some mutual exploration of a more intimate kind.

Back on the beach I splashed through the last few feet of water and loped up the slope to where Max knelt. He was piling palm fronds under a lean-to built with the boat and some pieces of driftwood.

"Hey, Max," I called as I ran; he turned and got the maximum effect of my jiggling breasts. It wasn't wasted on him.

"What's up?" he said, and then turned quickly back. I resisted commenting on the obvious.

"I found an oyster bed out there. Might be a little hard to get them down raw without lemon or Tabasco, but better than starving. And better than the rats they're eating back at the base." I tossed my prizes on the sand.

"I guess," he said, clearly not really focused on eating of that kind.

I moved closer, until my thigh was against his shoulder. "I don't suppose we'll be here long enough to worry about starvation, anyway. I find myself thinking more about things I'd really, really like to fit in while we're still here. Alone."

He'd pulled his shorts back on, but not his shirt. I leaned on his broad back and nuzzled his neck. He knelt there, unmoving, supporting my weight, until I began chewing lightly, teasingly, on his muscular shoulders. "Did you know that oysters can switch their sex?" I murmured against his rigid jaw.

"Lexie," he said, his deep voice getting even deeper, "what do you think you're doing?"

"If there's any doubt, I must not be doing it right." I brushed my nipples across his back and knew he could feel them harden.

"But I thought . . ."

"I know what you thought. And I know what you're thinking now. Drives you crazy, doesn't it, envisioning what women do with each other." I reached around his chest to flick his nipples; they sprang to attention. An interesting effect on hard muscle instead of soft curves.

"If it didn't before, it does now," he muttered. I worked one hand down inside his jeans, over the bunched muscles of his buttocks and then in between; suddenly he twisted under me and ended up on his back on the palm-leaf bed, with me astride.

"Damn it, Lexie," he growled, "you'd better be going somewhere with this!"

There's something about a deep, deep masculine voice. A woman's voice can be like a stroke on quivering flesh, like the warm, wet thrust of a tongue, but Max's voice set up reverberations so penetrating they seemed to liquefy my bones.

"Trust me," I assured him. "I never met an erogenous zone I couldn't appreciate." I rode the huge bulge in his pants, appreciating the hell out of it.

It was almost enough to get me off all by itself, but I had other plans. "Check me out, if you need proof." I lifted myself just enough for his hand to test my natural lube. His digital enthusiasm was touching, if a bit clumsy. I continued pursuing other interests, sliding backward until I had his zipper just far enough open to insert two fingers, then slowly, slowly widening the gap until my whole hand curved around his hot, hard cock, still trapped by the pressure of his belt.

His hips rose, his hands scrabbled at the belt buckle, and I leaned forward and caught the tip of his cock in my mouth as it jerked free.

I savored it for a while, with just enough in-out action to keep him breathing hard without rushing things. Then I leaned back and hitched my body along his until my knees clutched his hips. My own hips moved back and forth as my cunt lips and clit slid back and forth over his swollen, eager cock. Too bad, I reflected, not for the first time, that our sense of taste is limited to the mouths we eat with. And a taste was all I was going to get.

"Max," I said, pulling back, "you wouldn't happen to know what the Swiss Family Robinson used for condoms, would you?"

"No, damn it," he said. "They must have cut that part from the movie to get a 'G' rating."

"Don't worry." I played him with my hand, stroking from the root of his balls all the way up his shaft. "Just lie back and let me run this fuck."

"You're the boss," he said, his voice rising into a gasp. I had pressed my knuckle firmly below his scrotum and was working my thumb back toward his asshole.

"I'll bet you'd like something really kinky," I teased, "to tell your grandchildren when you get too old for anything but stories."

"I'll bet you have inside information," he said, not too steadily, "about what Robinson Crusoe used for sex toys!"

"Is that a challenge?" I watched a gleaming pearl of precum form at the slit in his cock. Perverse inspiration struck. "If so, I accept."

I yanked the belt from his shorts; he lifted his head in alarm but didn't try to stop me. His expression went from apprehension to uncertainty to horrified awe as I leaned over to grab the oysters.

The belt buckle was just the tool for prying open the very large, very tough shells. "No pearl in this one," I said, bringing the opened bivalve close to his erection. "Maybe you could share." I tapped his cock; it jerked. I just managed to catch his dewdrop on the oyster, while some of the liquid cupped in the shell dripped onto his balls. I bent to lick it off, then touched my tongue to the glistening shellfish.

"A good beginning, but it could use more sauce." I slid the oyster from the shell into my mouth and held it there, excitement balancing revulsion, while I worked Max hard, inexorably, with both hands. At the penultimate moment, when his deep moans began to rise in pitch and quicken until they nearly flowed together, I worked my mouth down over his cock. It was all I could do to keep the slippery oyster from being rammed down my throat, but I managed to wait until Max's storm of cries rattled my bones and the hot flood of his coming burst over my tongue.

Swallowing had never been quite like that before. The taste was indescribable. And unforgettable. It was a while before Max regained enough breath to speak. "Lexie," he said, "what about . . . It's your turn. . . ." I could tell he was trying not to look at the remaining oyster. I plucked it from its shell and cradled it in my palm. It was a very large, very juicy oyster. Liquid dripped between my fingers into my lap and seeped downward to join my own juices.

"No, it's your turn," I said, leaning back and spreading my legs. The oyster was cold against my tender heat; I tensed but kept pushing. Between its slippery coating and my own wet readiness, it went in easily. My cunt tried to grip the slick, yielding pressure, and the teasing subtlety of the stimulation began to drive me crazy. "It's your turn," I said, gasping, "to eat!"

"Well," Max said, "considering the gourmet dipping sauce. . . ." And he ate, his willingness to learn exceeded only by the length of his truly phenomenal tongue and the dexterity of his fingers on my breasts. It was a long time before I realized that the throbbing sounds filling the air weren't all coming from me.

"A search helicopter," Max said, and wiped his mouth.

"Damn," I said. I groped for the belt buckle and rolled over until I could reach inside the prow of the boat. I started gouging the already splintered wood around what seemed to be a bolt, until Max's large, dark hand covered mine and took the buckle and finished the job.

"How long have you known it was there?" he asked, when the tiny camera lay at last cupped in my hand.

"I noticed it this morning when I woke up," I said. "Want me to send you a copy of the tape, if I manage to smuggle it out?"

"You'd better," he said. "Not that I'm likely to forget any of it."

"Not as long as there are oyster bars in the world," I agreed.

"I don't think I'll be eating any more oysters," Max shouted over the increasing noise, "unless that special sauce comes with them."

"Sauce for the goose as well as the gander," I called, but, luckily, my voice was swallowed by the roar of the rotors. The chopper was so close now we could feel the wind. I scrabbled for my clothes.

From high above the little crescent of sand and rock seemed to smile in the liquid embrace of the ocean. The breakers along its outer curve hinted only at the fierce assault a storm could bring, while the lapping of the wavelets inside the lagoon kept up a gentle, relentless stimulation. I shifted in my seat in the helicopter, new waves of tingling overlapping the residual glow between my legs.

The camera was in my pocket. I knew where I could hide the tape later, if I had to, to get it home; I might even manage the whole miniature camera, if only briefly. I grinned to myself. Max probably thought I was thinking of him, which was fine, but I was really filled with images of how Tonya would get the most out of a cuntcam.

It was a damned shame, though, that she was allergic to seafood. ◆

DEPTHS

BY DAVE SMEDS

The airport on Grand Cayman teemed with tourists and vacationing businessmen outfitted in bright cotton-print shirts and shorts. Thomas spotted a chauffeur holding a cardboard sign bearing the name he was using on this trip, and wove his way through a sea of gratuity-keen baggage handlers to the limousine.

The chauffeur stowed the garment bag in the trunk. Thomas escaped the glare of tropical daylight for the sanctuary of the passenger compartment. Vanilla-scented currents of cool air breathed up from the vents, peeling away the grasp of the island atmosphere.

A bottle of Dom Perignon rested in a bucket of ice within easy reach of the best seat. Thomas popped the cork and poured himself a glass. The driver pulled away from the curb so smoothly the beverage scarcely wobbled.

First class was Monique's style, and she had the money to pull it off. The only thing missing was the presence of Monique herself. But rules were rules.

The limo carried him beyond George Town to a seaside villa nestled behind a high fence draped with lianas and mandevilla. The chauffeur placed the luggage and champagne on the flagstones of the front walkway and departed at once, not even momentarily posturing for a tip. Soon the purr of the vehicle faded back down the avenue. No one was left to see who greeted Thomas.

Thomas stepped through an arbor and turned down the path, the lane vanishing behind him. Now, at last, Monique appeared on the upper level of the house and leaned over the stone balustrade. When their eyes met, the radiance of her smile bewitched him as fully as it had the last time they had rendezvoused. That had been Maui, in January. Before that it was Raratonga in October, a mere two weeks after the night on the lake in Geneva.

The places didn't matter, except that each location, in its turn, provided the chance to be with Monique.

His gaze roved down her throat to the cleavage brimming out of her sundress. He adored watching her respond to the sight of him. A blush poured across her upper body. Her nipples rose, straining against the fabric. Heart revving up, he scampered up the steps.

They met inside the foyer. He flipped the door closed with his foot. The ritual was complete. For the next forty-eight hours, they would be in their own genie-bottle universe.

They embraced. She brought her lips up to his. Their tongues twined around each other. The butterfly that had come in with them fluttered all the way to the kitchen and back, and still they pressed against each other, savoring.

Finally they ended the kiss, if only to be able to look to each other's eyes.

"How was your flight?" she asked.

"Good. Quick." Anticipation had condensed the hours.

She stepped back, took his hand, and led him toward the master bedroom.

They postponed further words. They were sure to babble themselves hoarse later on, but words were a treasure they could share long-distance—on the cell phone her husband didn't know she owned, by email through her password-protected account. Now that they were finally up close, skin to skin, other needs took precedence.

The bed could have slept ten, but it was dwarfed by the palatial chamber. Subdued daylight filtered through the drapes, silhouetting a balcony replete with clay planters of bougainvillea. Inside, sachets of dried flowers on the nightstands perfumed the air. Thomas was not surprised to find the state-of-the-art sound system turned off. Monique preferred to make love against a background of murmuring water, of waves—in this case, those of the Caribbean surging against the rocks a dozen yards beyond the balcony. That and their own murmurs were the best possible music.

Monique pranced ahead, turning around as she reached the bed. Her grin spread from ear to ear. She wriggled out of the dress.

He paused to adore her nakedness. He knew she would forgive him the instant glance downward and the subsequent lingering scrutiny. A beach addict, the only pubic hair Monique permitted consisted of a sculpted triangle on her mons, a token badge of femininity tamed to fit within the confines of her skimpiest thong bikini bottom. Below that, not so much as a strand stood guard to block his access.

The tip of his tongue rose and begin massaging the inside of his lower lip. Rehearsing.

His glance rose back to her mouth. It was open, upturned, offered like fruit. He kissed her again.

Finally, she pressed him back. She grinned, this time wider still, though that hardly seemed possible.

She lay back on the mattress, spreading her legs. Her labia parted, blossoming, wetness already glinting upon the pink flesh she exposed.

He slid out of his clothes slowly. Her gaze roved over him. As her glance settled on the evidence of his arousal, her eyes sparkled.

He glided forward, kissed her lightly on the mouth, spent a few moments sucking each nipple from erect to engorged, and shifted down between her legs.

His tongue caressed her clitoris, rode down her right lip, then up the left, moistening as he went. She gasped, as vulnerable as ever to that clockwise stroke. He brushed lightly for the first few licks, then more fully. Her taste anointed his tongue.

"Oh, Thomas," she·murmured. Her hips writhed, but she kept the reaction under control, preferring not to interrupt his oral worship by bucking too high or suddenly.

Continuing to lightly tongue her nub, he explored lower down, wetting his thumb. Gently, without insistence, he began to rub. Her labia turned more elastic, more eager, with each caress. Finally he probed with his middle finger.

Monique gave a sudden intake of breath as he penetrated her. Her flesh began to quiver around his finger, which he left in, pressed against and kneading her right atop her pubic bone.

Some women, to his surprise, did not react to G-spot massage, but Monique always had. He vibrated his finger in place, letting the sensation travel up into her through the bone. Experience told him this, along with the licking, would soon bring her to one of her most all-encompassing sorts of climaxes.

He adopted a determined rhythm that let her know she was going to have to come before she would get any dick at all.

Her gasps and sighs said she understood.

He slid into a recollection of the first orgasm he had lured out of her. Had it really been three years ago?

Singapore.

He had assumed he wouldn't find much action in the Asian city, the most prudish he had ever lived in. He had expected to be deliriously grateful to end his three-month sojourn. That was before he met Monique, a marketing executive for the software company that had hired him to assist with the launch of their new graphics chip. And wife of the chairman of the board, as it happened, though she never used that fact to coerce her staff. She apparently preferred to show she could stand on her own, and her spouse remained back in the U.S., rarely mentioned and never present.

They worked together for weeks, often huddled in the same cubicle, testing to destruction what the engineers brought them. After hundreds of hours breathing her cologne, brushing elbows, leaning so close together he had memorized every contour of her earlobes, he was unable to resist.

"Would you like to have dinner to celebrate?" he asked.

She clicked her computer mouse, faxing to the U.S. headquarters the last of the documents they'd revised. The job was done. The next day she would be on a plane to the annual sales conference in Silicon Valley, and he would be packing up his

Singapore apartment for good. His next freelance assignment was already waiting for him back in Seattle.

"Yes," she said. "I would like that very much."

He had convinced himself her positive response must have been a daydream by the time he showed up at the rooftop restaurant overlooking Marina Bay, but there she was, in a shoulderless evening gown, emeralds dangling from those earlobes he had come to know so well.

"You clean up nice," he quipped. He had seen her in business suits and in a sweatshirt and drawstring pants. She looked gorgeous to him in any mode, but the evening held a difference. The aspect she wore now was that of a woman who wanted to make an impression.

The first half hour they discussed the menu, ordered, talked shop, pointed out favorite sights along the harbor vista.

"I love the water," Monique said. A seemingly neutral comment, but with a tone different than she had used for the small talk. Thomas wondered if it was a segue.

"So do I," he replied carefully. "My wife and I met on a sailboat."

Damn. He had not intended to mention his wife at all that evening.

"I imagine she will be glad to have you home."

He cleared his throat. "Actually, my coming to Singapore was our trial separation. We're getting divorced."

He had to sip his iced tea to quell his dry mouth. He had overheard women cursing all men who used the "I'm getting a divorce" line. He had not mentioned his impending lack of marriage to anyone here; he had no way to prove he was telling the truth.

"That's too bad," she responded.

"Yeah. Not much more to say." He sipped more tea. "How about you? Looking forward to seeing your husband?"

"Yes, of course."

She answered too quickly. He caught her glance.

"I adore my husband. I could never imagine being married to anyone else."

"I see."

"Were you hoping to seduce me tonight?" she asked.

Thomas nearly inhaled an ice cube. "Not . . . anymore. Until a few moments ago I was hoping there might be a chance. But don't worry. I know how to gracefully accept defeat."

He prepared to adopt the role of a gentleman for the remainder of the evening, but Monique did not have the look of a woman putting up shields.

"Give me your foot," she asked.

"Pardon?"

She gestured reassuringly. He lifted his foot beneath the table. She reached beneath the tablecloth, slipped off his shoe and sock. . .

. . . And tucked his foot between her legs, under her gown.

He explored and found that she had shifted the crotch of her panties to the side. Unobstructed, his toes nudged rubbery flesh. She was wet.

No. She was *drenched.*

"That's how much I want you," she said.

He hesitated. Afraid to say anything for fear the wrong response would mean having to move his toes away from her wetness, her heat.

"Are you teasing me?" he asked faintly.

"I don't tease. You can have me tonight if you want." She squeezed her thighs together, trapping his foot amid the slick spot. She closed her eyes and sighed. "As long as we understand eachother."

Not a tease? He was already erect, but the promise hardened him to the point of twitching.

"I'm an understanding guy," he replied. "Talk to me."

"My husband is an incredible man. Mature. Civilized. Charming."

"But . . . ?"

"He's older. His sex drive was always much lower than mine, but I told myself that didn't matter. The marriage is so ideal in other ways that I made do with the little I got in bed. But in the past couple of years his libido has fallen to a level so much below mine I've had to do all the asking."

"That's got to be depressing." Thomas couldn't imagine any man being uninterested in having sex with Monique. Was there something he wasn't seeing?

"I'm strong. I can cope as long as he keeps saying yes. And he does. The problem is, if I have to be any more assertive than I have been, it'll cross the line and become begging."

"No one should have to do that. Not on a regular basis," Thomas declared.

"I can handle it. That is, I can handle it as long as I know I'm worthy of the sex."

"For Christ's sake, why wouldn't you be?"

She brightened at his outrage, the first glimmer of a smile since she had broached the stressful topic. "You see, that's the information I need to have. Is it me? Have I somehow become . . . unappealing?"

"The self-image thing," Thomas stated.

"You do understand." Her voice quavered. "I've started to doubt myself. I need a second opinion. I've come to know you well enough over these past weeks that I know I can trust you to tell me the truth, good or bad."

"Of course," he promised.

"In the morning, I'll go back to my married life," she added. "I'm talking one-night stand. Not an affair. I just need to step outside my vows long enough to *know*."

"I can live with that. Thanks for being aboveboard."

"You don't mind being used?"

"Use me," he said.

They skipped dessert and retreated to her penthouse. She was perfectly ladylike in the taxicab and elevator, but in her foyer, she turned from locking the door, seized him by his shirtfront, and planted her lips fiercely against his.

One thing was certain—there was nothing deficient in her kissing. Thomas was perspiring when their mouths finally separated. Pressed up against one another, they gazed into each other's eyes from lovers' distance apart.

What now?

Rip each other's clothes off and do it on the carpet? Have a drink and proceed through foreplay rituals one careful stage at a time? Being so close to Monique brought up all of Thomas's usual first-time-with-someone concerns. Had he shaved closely enough before dinner? Was food stuck in his teeth?

Piss on the doubts. They were just details to get in the way. Except, perhaps, for one. He was still sweaty from the kiss, from the anticipation as they rode in the taxi, from the humid Singapore streets. He didn't want to be concerned about body odor.

That was a problem easily dealt with, though. "Want to begin with a shower?" he suggested.

"I think that sounds great." Suddenly she was no longer blushing, no longer casting her glance downward in bashfulness. He realized he had said exactly the right thing to put her at ease.

She took his hand and led him to the bathroom with casual grace. They undressed together with an equally natural flair, like a couple who had done this together many times before—she slipping his trousers onto a hanger, he helping her with the zipper of her gown.

Beneath the calm, traces of behavior betrayed their eagerness. His breath caught as her breasts were revealed. She murmured appreciatively when his cock, already well on the way to full mast, reacted to liberty from its wrappings. Yet they avoided touching each other in an overtly sexual way until they had stepped beneath the spray.

She rotated slowly beneath the nozzle, soaking down, then let him do the same. While his eyes were closed, he felt her begin washing his back. When that was done, she pressed up against him and reached around him to continue with his front. That brought her skin to skin at last. He savored the delicious, tactile presence of her breasts pancaking against his shoulder blades, her belly nudging his lower back.

She soaped up his genitals, but though her hands lingered on his erection, squeezing it fondly, he sensed she was just playing, enjoying the intimacy, not yet "having sex." Sure enough, she continued downward, continuing to wash him. When she reached his ankles, she helped him rinse off, then she held out the bar of soap.

He took it and paused. The shower had completed the transformation he had noted at the beginning of the evening. Makeup gone, hair suspended in long, drenched strands absent of any styling or hairspray, the co-worker had disappeared. Monique was all woman now. Not an executive. Not a dinner companion. The water had revealed her as herself.

She turned. He washed her back, rinsed it, and then pressed up against her as she had done to him. His erection found a welcome in the hollow at the base of her spine, in the upper juncture of her rump cheeks. Monique was only a trifle shorter than he. They fit well.

She sighed as he ran his soapy hands over her breasts. He continued downward, wondering whether he should be as thorough at her crotch as she had been with him. But she parted her legs, welcoming his exploration.

He fondled her with a solicitous, don't-get-suds-inside expertise and, as he set the bar aside and softly rubbed away its traces, realized by the shuddering of her spine against his abdomen what a hair-trigger state she was in.

She melted against him, held up less by her own legs than by his hands, one of which cupped her near the navel, the other which continued to caress and probe her recesses. That hand was slick not with water or soap but with her secretions. He kneaded in a small circle, pushing her folds around in a steady but never quite predictable pattern.

"I . . . I . . ." she began to say. To give him advice? Encouragement? Or just to proclaim her readiness to come? Her words were rinsed away and became incoherent, animal murmurs of joy.

She shuddered, body pushing against him as the orgasm flowed upward, and sagging against him as each wave of clenching eased. The sounds produced by her throat alternated between heaves and sharp, severe catching of her breath. Thomas wasn't sure he had ever encountered a woman so ready, and so responsive, to his touch. It inspired him so much that the touch of her slick buns and lower spine against his hard-on was almost too much to bear without spurting.

Monique opened her eyes, sighed, and, beaming at him in gratitude, caught the desperation in his aura.

"Looks like we both need to take the edge off," she said. "That's okay with you?"

"It'll let us take our time later." She grinned and knelt down in front of him.

He gasped as her mouth engulfed him. She wasted no time applying herself. She wanted his pleasure. The water beat down on her head and poured down her face in rivulets, coursing over the juncture of her lips and his cock, two types of hot wetness anointing him, simultaneously and yet also in alternation.

His breathing deepened. Tingles began deep in his pelvis. He silently thanked the fates that he didn't have to hold back. No man who had been deprived as long as he could have resisted the determined milking action of her tongue and cheeks.

He moaned as the pulses roared up his cock. Somehow his knees managed not to give way. Monique was an angel, keeping the stimulation steady and uninterrupted until he had spent his last drop.

He was so delirious he didn't even notice when she shut off the faucet and stood up. He opened his eyes to find himself gazing into her face. She wore a mischievous, proud grin.

He chuckled and wrapped his arms around her, holding her so close the hug wrung out the droplets that had dotted the fronts of their bodies. As he inhaled, she exhaled. As she exhaled, she inhaled. Even catching up on their oxygen supply had become a shared enterprise—another way to make love.

"Monique," he said when he had regained his breath, "it's not you. Whatever is keeping your husband disinterested—it's not you."

She beamed at him. "You haven't actually *fucked* me yet, good sir. How can you tell?"

He chuckled. "You're right. I'll report back after I've done more research."

It was absolutely true, of course. Monique was inherently fuck-able. And by the time Thomas had said good-bye to her at the airport the next day, the wiggle in her hips and the way her chin rode high in the air proclaimed how thoroughly she believed his assessment. Over the course of the night they had made love twice more—intercourse, and in bed, no less. He had smelled her pheromones. He had held her close. She knew he was telling the truth.

He went home knowing he had given her a gift, and was proud of it. He also went taking her at her word that she would hold to her course and look back on their encounter as an isolated incident. Women were like that. They could have mind-blowing sex with a guy and pass up the chance for an encore.

Except that Monique had changed her mind. A few months after Singapore, after his divorce had gone through and he was floating sexually adrift, wondering when romance would reenter his life, she had dropped him a line in email. Within another week they were talking on the phone daily. A month later came the first rendezvous, in Brighton.

And now here he was, his flesh once again enveloped by hers, as it had been for most of the past hour, in one position or another. On her back, breathless from her athletic efforts of the past few minutes, she pulled her knees up high and let him do the work. She was sure to be sore in the morning, but her openmouthed glow of ecstasy as he thrust told him she was willing to pay the price.

He leaned back, legs folded, rump nearly resting on his heels, so that his hands no longer had to support his weight. He kneaded her clit with his thumb. Using cock and hand simultaneously was one of the lovemaking options her husband had never made a habit of—even back when he was providing her with regular sexual attention.

"Yes," she purred, whether in appreciation that he had resorted to one of their private techniques, or simply because it was giving her such tingles. Either way was fine with him.

He could tell she was going to come again. She couldn't help it. And neither, by this time, could he.

He poured into her just at the moment her nostrils began to vacuum in sharp doses of air. He gave her the load he had been storing up for the previous three days.

When they came back to their senses, Monique began to giggle. He understood without explanation. They were so sopping wet it was funny. He expected there would be long discussions later about who would get to sleep in the wet spot.

Assuming they got any sleep.

She had learned from their previous encounters, though. As they uncoupled, she leaned over and opened a nightstand drawer. She pulled out a hand towel, which she stuffed between her legs so that she wouldn't have to interrupt the sweetness of the afterglow by leaving the bed. Instead they lingered on their sides, spooning, bodies pressed close, lower legs overlapping.

The question that had been incubating in Thomas's mind worked its way back to the forefront of his thoughts. Now was the perfect time to bring up the subject. Namely, them. Their relationship.

Yet Thomas hesitated. Three years they had been lovers. In that time, they had not discussed their status with each other beyond the planning required to arrange their trysts. Did he really want to discuss when and if things would ever change?

The words he had been considering retreated back to their niche. Only a fool would risk what he had.

"Something on your mind?" Monique asked. "You seem distracted."

"It's nothing," he said. "Forget it. I'm back in the moment."

"Good," she said, and stretched like a cat against him. "Because I was just thinking that was not bad for a warm-up."

Thomas mirrored her grin. She had a point. Forty-seven hours to go. They were just getting started.

So what if he saw her only two or three times a year? So what if their time together was carved off of the rest of their lives and compartmentalized? He would be a sailor on that ocean, as long as she waited at each port of call. ◆

SHELTER FROM THE STORM

BY CHRIS JONES

Leather keeps you dry. At least that's what I'd told myself when I'd set out to walk the ten blocks to the bar. And it might have been true if I hadn't been walking on a blustery September night through the tail end of a hurricane. They've usually petered out by the time they get this far north, but this one was still plenty wet and plenty windy.

The wind was so bad, I'd taken off my cap and rain was pouring over my head, running down my face and neck, infiltrating the leather to soak my T-shirt. Unavoidable puddles were inundating my socks. What had ever possessed me to go out in weather like this?

Horniness. There was no other answer. I needed sex bad, and I was hoping on a night like this there'd be a few other intrepid souls at the bar who needed it as much as I did. But I was only halfway there, and I already looked like shit. By the time I got there, I'd be thoroughly wet and in no mood to cruise.

I was about to head back home when I caught sight of the abandoned warehouse. I'd heard stories about some heavy sex going on in there, but of course I'd never checked it out. Given a choice, I'll take a place with central heating and plumbing. But maybe tonight I'd try something rougher. If I couldn't find a partner, I could at least get off to someone else's scene. That's assuming anyone was there at all.

I clambered over the fence that secured the small lot attached to the building. I think you're supposed to wriggle under it, but the obvious place to do that was practically a stream. Besides, I was unlikely to be noticed on a night like this. I made my way around the back and found a door, still hasped and bolted on one side, but hanging crazily from its hinges on the other. I squeezed my way through.

It was like walking into a different universe. Dry and still, only the faint sound of the rain drumming on the roof high overhead—which was way too quiet for me. No sound of leather on flesh, no groans, no moans, not even heavy breathing. Well, it had been a long shot. At least I was out of the rain. Maybe I'd stay awhile and hope the storm slacked off. I could at least check the place out for some future scene.

Although my eyes were fairly well adjusted, it was still pretty dark in the back near the door. The front section seemed to be better lit, perhaps by a streetlight shining through an unboarded window. I headed in that direction.

Strewn on the floor was the typical detritus of male sexual

space anywhere: condoms, gloves, empty lube containers. As I got closer to the lighted area, I could see other things, like strategically placed nails where ropes could be slung or tied, and pallets and crates stacked so that bottoms could be thrown over them and fucked. Someone had even left an air mattress. I gave one crate a kick to see how sturdy it was.

"Ed, is that you?"

I whirled around and saw something fleshy-looking tied to a pillar close to the light source. So there was some action going on tonight. I stepped closer.

Blindfolded and trussed was a guy I'd seen a couple times in the bars. The tops were calling him Whiny Guy. I'd heard he had a tendency to safeword a lot, ending scenes with everyone unsatisfied. Right now he was in what I call inverted Y position: arms bound together and tied over his head, legs spread. Tit clamps, chained together, hung from his nipples, and his cock was partially hard. It was a nice picture, one I would have liked seeing animated. That is, if his top didn't throw me out.

"Look, Ed, I'm sorry I safeworded. I was afraid you were going to whip my cock." He stopped, swallowed, and grabbed a breath. "Maybe you are. I . . ." Another break for air. "If that's what you want, go ahead." He tensed himself for the blow.

I looked around. Where the hell was Ed? You never, ever leave a bottom trussed and then get out of earshot. Unless it was Ed Lapent. He was irresponsible enough to leave someone who'd safeworded tied up alone for a couple of hours "to teach him a lesson." Sometimes, if they were lucky, they learned not to pick tops just for their looks. But sometimes they took other lessons home, like distrust and paranoia and lots of anger. Things that made it worse for everyone.

So much for playing tonight. The only thing to do was untie him and make sure he was okay. Take him out for coffee, let him vent, try to get him to figure out how not to have this happen again.

It was too bad. He was just set to give in and let his top take him somewhere he'd never thought of going. It was the part of S/M that I find most deeply arousing. Maybe I could just take off my belt and . . .

I stopped my fantasy, dug the pocketknife out of my pants, and stepped up to him.

He gasped. "Oh, God, that's cold." I hadn't even touched him. Then I saw water dripping off his forehead and flowing around his nose. I looked up. A small stream of water was falling from above. The ceiling must have sprung a leak.

The water ran off his close-clipped beard and onto his chest. He should have been thrashing, trying to get his head away from the icy water, but he didn't. He just stood there letting it cascade over him.

"Is this right, Ed? Is this what you want?" His breathing was ragged and his cock was getting harder. I drew a breath myself as a sharp shiver of excitement raced down my body. He was going to surrender. Right here, to no one in particular, just the forces of nature and the circumstances that he found himself in. I could cut him down and ruin the moment. I could introduce myself and watch his excitement ebb as I tried to renegotiate the scene. Or I could also give in to the circumstances I was presented with. I put the knife away.

"Yeah. That's what I want." I said it low, leaning over him, practically on top of his ear. With that I gave his shoulder a hard push to the left and watched the water head down over his pec and hit his nipple clamp. He jerked away hard as the cold seeped into the metal, no doubt sending new signals up his abused nerves. I forced him back into position. This time he stayed, moaning and squirming but taking it.

Using my tongue, I followed the line of water down through his dark chest hair, warming the channel the water ran through. When I got to the nipple I ringed the aureole and then took the clamp with its squeezed flesh in my mouth, warming it thoroughly. When I left I gave the chain just a tweak, producing a whimper from my victim.

I continued to follow the water as it coursed down his abs and on down his leg, just missing his cock and balls. He was cut, his shaft rising from a ring of wiry, dark curls. I wanted to taste it but contented myself with inhaling his scent as I dragged my tongue along his inner hip.

I continued down his thigh and finally left off at the knee. On the way back up I used my hands. I found belt burns on the front of his thighs. I rubbed them hard to reawaken them. Moving my hands around to the back, I found a weal on his inner thigh. I kneaded it lightly and then moved up over his buttocks. They were covered with marks. And with my hands on his cheeks, I knew why. He had that perfect kind of ass that I love to watch flinch away from a belt and then stick itself back out, begging for more. I pinched him and was rewarded, after an initial pulling away, by him relaxing into my hand, silently begging me for abuse. I obliged while watching his cock, curving upward in that aching arc of need. I was swollen, too. I opened my coat, undid my belt, and pulled down my zipper so I could get at myself.

"Fuck me, Ed." He must have heard the zipper.

I'd forgotten about Ed. Now what? Where I wanted to go with this scene was not the sort of thing Ed Lapent would ever do. Was my bottom going to freak on me when he figured it out? I reflected for a moment. Not if he was really *my* bottom, he wasn't. He was going to go wherever I took him. And I was going to make it a place very, very different from what he expected.

I stripped off my shoes and pants—they were just in the way now—and moved my knife to my jacket pocket. Quickly I slung the air mattress over a pallet. Next I cut him down and pushed him over to the makeshift bed, where I toppled him gently onto it. I retrieved the rope that had bound his arms and cut it in four sections. He spread his arms for me, and as I tied him, he lifted his legs, ready for fucking. But I gave them a yank and tied them down as well.

Then, kneeling over him, I pulled the lube out of my pocket, squeezed a tiny drop out and watched it fall, in that slow viscous way that water-based lubes do, onto his cock. He jerked, thinking no doubt it was more rainwater, but I had my hand on him, spreading the lube, getting him hard, keeping him focused on the physical. I had two fingers of my other hand up my own ass, loosening it up. God, I wanted his cock. I had the condom on him and lubed before he knew it was out of the package, and straddling him, I sat on him hard and quick. I usually like it slower, but I didn't want him thinking at all.

As he bucked up to meet me on the second thrust, I thought I might have succeeded, but then I saw his face change. "You're not Ed." It wasn't a question.

I pulled myself off, hanging above him, just out of reach. "Do you care?" I hissed. His hips were moving involuntarily, butting the tip of his penis up against my ass.

He moaned, "No," and tried to get in me again, but I kept myself just out of reach.

"Beg for it." It was a growl.

I saw his lips form the F for fuck, but then he realized that was wrong. Finally he blurted out, "Take me."

And I did. There's no better reward for a bottom who gets it right. And finally, with his dick firmly engulfed in my ass, I touched myself. I was slick and wet and my clit felt like it was going to explode any minute. I cupped myself with my palm, bouncing against it as I thrust down on his cock, but even that was too much. I pulled my hand away.

I turned my attention to my bottom, squeezing him a little and getting a moan. That was good, but I didn't want us to come yet. I wanted to ride that hard cock, make it wet with precum and need. The way I was going to be wet when I touched myself again.

That's when I remembered the nipple clamps. I caressed the chain; his mouth tightened, knowing what I planned, and his thrusts became frenzied. Riding him low so he could get in deep with his limited range of movement, I gripped the chain, resting my fist on his chest, its wiry hair rough on my knuckles. His cock pounded my ass. I felt as if it were swelling with each thrust, almost bursting. Now! I pulled the clamps off. He screamed, his face distorting in pain and ecstasy, and started coming. Dropping the chain, I rammed my hand against my clit and followed his movements down into that timeless moment of bliss.

A little later he shifted under me. "My God, that was amazing. Who the hell are you?"

I got off him, the drag of his spent cock on my ass reawakening my desire. He thought the scene was over. Would he go any further with me? I savored the cusp of discovery while I pulled my pocket knife out. I opened it, quickly cut his bonds, and put it away. He immediately reached for the blindfold, but I pinned his arms down with a knee across his chest.

"Come on, let me see." Whiny Guy was reasserting himself. A bad sign. Putting him off wasn't going to make it any more interesting. I pulled the blindfold off.

"Shit, you're a girl!" He tried to sit up.

I put my weight on his chest and leaned over him so I was eye to eye with him. "I'm a top. You call me Sir." But he wrenched away.

I let him get up. You can only take people where they want to go.

"Did Ed put you up to this?" He sounded more confused than angry. Which was good. Maybe I could get him to see what had happened, where he'd taken himself.

I retrieved my pants and started to climb into them. "Ed left you tied up by yourself. I stumbled in by accident, just as the water hit you from the ceiling leak."

He was scrambling around looking for the clothes he'd shed so long ago. "He wouldn't leave me."

Shit, he wasn't listening.

He found his shirt and pulled it on. "He put you up to this. He probably watched the whole thing. Now he'll tell everyone I do girls."

I was being dismissed as a prop in an Ed Lapent scenario! I grabbed my shoes and sat down on the pallets to put them on. What was I going to do? I should be apologizing for not getting his consent, helping him to process all the things he'd been through. But I wasn't even real enough to him to hold his attention. I watched him put on his pants, muttering under his breath. All I caught was "breasts" and "disgusting."

I finished tying my shoes and stood up. "If you don't like what Ed does, don't play with him."

He didn't even look up from putting his pants on. I zipped my coat and went back out into the rain. ◆

NUMBER FOURTEEN

BY SIMON SHEPPARD

The Soviet submarine slices silently through the waters of New York Harbor.

The Communist commander is peering through the periscope . . . at the Statue of Liberty! "We shall destroy," he sneers, "this symbol of America—and all she stands for." There's a very evil grin on his face.

Meanwhile . . . on Bedloe's Island, a high school field trip stands at the foot of the Statue. Philip MacReady, just turned eighteen, lifts his Brownie to his eye.

". . . will ever stand as a symbol of the American way . . ." the teacher is saying.

A device in Philip MacReady's ear emits a secret signal from his mentor. The students make their way toward the Statue's entrance, but young MacReady hangs back from the group.

The Soviet sailor's face is contorted by hate. "Ready the missiles, comrades! We shall DESTROY HER!!"

"Captain! Look! On the underwater television-scope!"

An awesomely familiar shape is streaking at jet speed toward the Soviet sub.

"Suffering Stalin! It's SeaScout!!!"

Kevin looked at himself in the full-length mirror. Not bad, really. Mid-thirties, just a bit of a belly. His dick was on the small side, but some guys liked small dicks. His face wasn't bad, though his ears stuck out a bit and he was getting the beginnings of a double chin. He would never pass for a superhero, but he was okay.

Enough—he had to quit daydreaming. It was a big day—some kid named Jeromy was bringing him a copy of *SeaScout Comics #14.* His collection would be complete.

SeaScout #14 had been published before Kevin McHugh was born. It had originally been his much older brother's, one of a big pile of comic books in the basement; Mike had left them behind when he went off to Vietnam and never came back. Sprawled on a shabby old sofa, Kevin had devoured every garishly colored page. There were the science fiction comics, the ones where square-jawed scientists fought off bug-eyed monsters while their buxom girlfriends cowered in a corner. The deliciously gory horror comics dripping with guts. There were a few soldier comics, too. And then there were the superheroes. Kevin had especially liked the superheroes: Captain America, Superman, the less popular ones like the Blue Beetle.

And SeaScout.

Mike had collected all the *SeaScout Comics,* all the way back to *SeaScout #1,* which featured a cover drawing of SeaScout thrusting upward from the waves, silhouetted against the New

York skyline, fist upraised, all supple strength and American courage. Atlantic foam gushed around his powerful body. Seawater coursed over his chiseled half-naked chest and muscular belly, swirling around his astonishing thighs. His formfitting costume, aqua blue and sea green, accentuated every rippling curve. There was even the suggestion of an erect nipple. Only his crotch remained hidden, the merest suggestion of bulk.

THE BIRTH OF A SUPERHERO! the cover exclaimed. And, in a dialogue balloon, SeaScout shouted his soon-to-be-famous call to action: "Sail ON!"

"Sail ON!" commands SeaScout, and the ocean itself leaps to respond. Waves begin to churn, underwater currents rise to typhoon strength. The Soviet sub is tossed about like a bathtub toy. Volcanoes sprout from the sea floor, belching lava with a ROARRR! And, amazingly, the tights-clad hero hoists the entire Commie warship above his head, heaved skyward on a gigantic waterspout.

The bearded captain, looking suspiciously like Lenin, spits out, "Curse you, SeaScout! Fire the warheads!" Two missiles flare forth from the ship, only to spiral wildly and head off harmlessly into space. But . . .

"The force of the missiles has knocked me off balance!" cries SeaScout to no one in particular. The sub begins to wobble, and SeaScout starts to plummet toward the ocean.

Of all the comic books in his brother's collection, the *SeaScout*s were Kevin's favorites. He'd loved the elemental strangeness of it all, how Rick Roman, a navy research scientist whose atomic experiment had been sabotaged by the Reds and gone horribly wrong, could command the mighty ocean itself. And then there was the way he looked, his bulging yet streamlined muscles flexing beneath the sea-colored costume.

When summer came and his family went to the public pool down the road, Kevin would imagine himself clad in clinging blue tights as he dove beneath the chlorinated surface, held his breath till his lungs were close to bursting, then pushed off from the turquoise-painted concrete of the pool bottom, shouting, as he soared into the muggy July sky, "Sail ON!"

"Can't . . . hold . . . on . . ." gasps SeaScout. *And then—miraculously—the sub rights itself, lofted skyward again. It's Flip, SeaScout's teenage sidekick, holding up the vessel's stern, steadying the Red sub. He's shown up in the nick of time. And now it rings out from them both, their rallying cry: "Sail ON!"*

Inside the lead sub, panicked sailors grab on to anything in a futile effort to save themselves, the commander frozen wide-eyed in fear.

And, at SeaScout's gesture, the ocean floor itself opens up, split by a huge, yawning fissure that sucks the lava, the submarine, everything but SeaScout and Flip deep, deeper, down into the bowels of the Earth.

By the time Kevin left for college, the simple "Good always triumphs" worldview of fifties comic books had been replaced in the public's fancy by the darker, more neurotic stories in the Marvel canon. Kevin would get stoned and read the latest about Spiderman's self-doubt and the mutant bonding of the X-Men. Something in him, though, still longed for the stories of SeaScout he'd left behind in the basement.

Kevin graduated from college just before his mother moved out of the house on Oakdale Road. Kevin's father had dumped her, remarried, and she, left on her own in the suburbs, was bored to distraction. Kevin had one last chance to rescue his childhood relics before she moved to a condo in Atlanta.

The SeaSub glides into its subterranean dock. Flip and SeaScout clamber out.

They get into the private high-speed elevator that shoots them upward to their penthouse, high above the city. "Another job well done, Flip." SeaScout lays a powerful hand on young Philip MacReady's shoulder. The elevator doors glide open and the two superheroes, arms around each other, walk down the marble-paneled hallway.

"It's time for bed, Philip." SeaScout turns, and, gazing out the window at the city lights far below, strips off the top of his costume. His back is broad and well muscled. Flip can see the semitransparent reflection of the older man's muscular torso in the window, V-shaped, perfect.

He'd gone down to the basement first thing. The comics were still there. Most of them were now valuable collectors' items, but they still sat there in a couple of raggedy corrugated-cardboard cartons. All except *SeaScout #14*, the rarest of the bunch. That one had somehow been left lying on the floor, and at some point the water heater had sprung a leak. The comic, what was left of it, was a water-damaged mess—its pages were wrinkled, the front cover spotted with mold, the last few pages stuck to the floor. It was not only worthless; the end of the story was totally unreadable. Stranded midway in the badly damaged comic, Kevin had invented the end of the story.

Flip walks over to SeaScout, now naked, standing at the window.

"Rick?" asks Flip, using SeaScout's given name. He lays his hand on the naked flesh of SeaScout's powerful shoulder.

"Philip, don't."

"But Rick . . . all this time together . . . I mean, how much longer can I stand this torture?"

"Philip, you're stronger than this." SeaScout is still staring out the window, out at the night. "We both are."

A tear falls from Flip's eye, leaving a salty trail on his cheek.

The years passed, flipping over like illustrated pages. Kevin, now in a low-level high-tech job at Princeton, got married; nothing special, the kind of thing you do because that's what's expected of you. Then, somewhere along the line, he discovered he liked to have sex with men. The divorce had been friendly but final, and since then Kevin's romantic life had been basically nonexistent. He didn't think of himself as "bi," exactly, much less "gay," but when he got horny he would, from time to time, head out to a dirty bookstore, where some stranger in a Lysol-soaked video booth would blow him. No muss, no fuss, no big deal. As his granny had said, in a slightly different context, "In the dark, all cats are black."

And there *were* those memories of SeaScout. . . .

Suddenly, there's a shattering of glass. Four men with gas masks over their faces—Soviet soldiers—burst through the broken picture window, propelled by rocket-packs strapped to their backs.

Clouds of noxious gas swirl through the penthouse. Within moments, the men carry the unconscious forms of Flip and the naked SeaScout out through the broken window, out into the night.

For years he'd let his comic book collection, carefully repackaged to reflect its amazingly high value, remain in storage, untouched. Then Kevin had had an astonishingly vivid dream about SeaScout. He—Kevin—had been Flip, and they had, the two of them, he and SeaScout, been swimming, effortlessly, weightless in azure seas. They circled, touched, whirled like dolphins, rubbed against each other, magnificent.

Kevin awoke to a damp spot in his bed; he'd had his first wet dream since high school.

It was then he'd taken his *SeaScout Comics* collection out of storage, complete except for #14, which had mildewed and rotted and finally been thrown away. He resolved, for old times' sake, to somehow get his hands on a copy of the rare missing issue. Number fourteen.

Kevin placed ads on a couple of Internet news groups, but *SeaScout #14* wasn't the easiest comic to come by. Amid the anticomics frenzy of 1950s America, renowned Dr. So-and-so had warned Congress about the "harm that comics could do," waving a copy of *SeaScout #14* and railing against the cleverly coded perversion contained therein. The writer of *SeaScout*, a right-wing Republican, protested that he, in fact, hated sex perverts every bit as much as he hated Commies, but to no avail. Though *SeaScout Comics #14* was already on the stands, the publisher recalled the copies that remained unsold and mulched them all, thereby courageously protecting America's youth from the unspeakable.

Flip comes to. He's lying on his back, firmly trussed up, tied down to a table in some dark dungeon. He turns his head and sees . . .

"Rick!" SeaScout is tied spread-eagle to a wall, arms and legs outstretched against cold concrete, a web of ropes bindng him to hooks set into the stone. He's still naked, though a small scrap of cloth drapes modestly across his crotch.

Flip struggles against the ropes, but in vain. He's firmly tied down, all right.

A green-painted metal door in a corner slides open, and a long shaft of light shoots across the floor.

"And now, SeaScout," says a man silhouetted in the doorway, "you shall see what lies in store for those who seek to foil the will of the working class!"

Kevin had started fantasizing about SeaScout often. After a hard day at work, he would fill the tub, light some candles, and slip into a hot bath, imagining that SeaScout was there with him, that Kevin had taken Flip's place, that he *was* Flip, he and SeaScout playing beneath the waves, swimming weightless among endless reefs of coral, forests of seaweed, the simple colors of comic books transformed by the tides of desire. SeaScout's aqua-colored costume just barely concealed a hard-on of titanic proportions, and Kevin glided up to it, his hands grasping its underwater heft, working it free. It was, of course, magnificent, the killer whale of pricks, arching toward the eerie blue sunlight that filtered from the surface far above. Kevin took it into his mouth. It tasted of brine and legend, and it filled his mouth as no other cock ever could. Together, he and SeaScout spiralled in a subaqueous dance of lust, in timeless blue space, startling the fish, trailing bubbles in their wake, until Kevin's hand, lubed with soap, coaxed an orgasm out of his own hard cock, salty white spurts that arced upward and landed in the bathwater, for a moment leaving little trails like the stuff in Lava Lamps, only to disperse, fluid into fluid, and be no more.

SeaScout squirms against his restraints. The little piece of cloth flutters to the floor.

"You won't get away with this!" Flip's face is contorted with anger, drops of sweat popping from his forehead.

"Ah, but on the contrary, we surely will." The Russian is dressed in an elegantly tailored suit, and he fairly purrs. "Face it, little fishy, you've been hooked."

He'd contacted Jeromy through an online newsgroup for comic book collectors. "SeaScout #14, anyone?" Jeromy's posting had read. No price was mentioned, just the words "not greedy." Kevin had sent an email to the poster and had been astonished when, a day later, a response appeared in Kevin's in box offering to sell him *SeaScout #14* for a mere fraction of what had been demanded on the online auction sites. At $500, Jeromy was asking far, far below fair value. It made Kevin suspicious.

"Can we talk by phone?" his response had read. When Jeromy called—a nineteen-year-old kid, it turned out—his doubts were put to rest . . . almost. Jeromy even lived in Jersey, too, not very far away.

"The comic book was my dad's. He died last year, and I gave most of his collection to charity. That's what he would have wanted; he was a generous guy. But . . . well, I could use a little money right now. I feel funny about selling any of his books at all; he always said that money was the worst reason to collect comics."

"You gave away his collection?"

"Yeah, I did. But I knew this *SeaScout* thing was the most valuable comic he had."

"You gave away his collection."

"Comic books don't mean very much to me. Sorry."

"Did you read *#14?*"

"Yeah," said Jeromy, "it wasn't bad."

The Russian walks over to SeaScout and takes the long cigarette holder from his mouth, bringing it close to SeaScout's naked chest. The Russian looks over at the tied-down teenager. "First we shall take care of you, little Flip, and then we'll deal with your . . . friend."

He touches the glowing cigarette to SeaScout's pec, and the superhero's face contorts in pain. There's a smell of scorched flesh.

"You Commie bastards!" Flip shouts. He stares at his naked hero and gets a shock. Could it be that SeaScout finds this situation . . . exciting?!?

After the phone call, Kevin started having ideas, kind of crazy ideas. Ideas about, well, about this boy Jeromy becoming his very own sidekick.

Kevin tried to imagine what it would be like. He'd lie back on the sofa in the dark, stroking his dick, imagining the two of them, Kevin and Jeromy, being buddies like SeaScout and Flip. Superheroes, two superheroes, floating side by side through the night. He'd never had a more intense fantasy; nothing had ever made his cock harder, more sensitive to his touch, more ready to gush a load of cum.

SeaScout and Flip. Kevin and Jeromy. Gliding through an underwater world. Swimming around each other, their costumes soaked through, becoming translucent, transparent, vanishing altogether, the two of them circling around eachother, naked beneath the sea, swimming closer and closer, stiff cocks like twin dolphins that finally rubbed up against each other, hard, wet flesh against hard, wet flesh.

And when he thought of that, Kevin would squeeze his dick just a bit harder, until the wave was inevitable, juices splashing across his naked chest. Once the spasms subsided, he'd rub his hand over the dampness that covered his chest and bring it to his mouth. It tasted like seawater.

"And now we shall see how long you can survive underwater, my young nemesis," the Red agent sneers. "Guards, prepare the room!"

Half a dozen Russian soldiers deploy themselves around the concrete cubicle. Metal shutters drop down over the walls. A drain in the center of the floor is sealed off. A light goes on in the middle of one wall; it's coming from a window into an adjoining cubicle.

"Now, SeaScout, prepare to watch your little guppy drown. There's not a thing you'll be able to do about it except shut your eyes, and even then," he takes a puff of his cigarette, "you'll be able to hear him scream."

The doorbell rang. It was Jeromy; no one else would be coming to the door this late, nearly eleven. Jeromy was a waiter at a seafood restaurant, of all places, and worked nights. And now, after his shift, he was bringing by, as arranged, a copy of *SeaScout #14* that, Kevin hoped, was the genuine article, the object of his desire.

As he walked toward the door, Kevin's dick shot upward, instantly hard. He'd expected that might happen and so he'd put on an oversize T-shirt and tight briefs under baggy pants, but as he opened the door, he still felt self-conscious.

Jeromy. Jeromy was a . . . surprise. He'd expected someone who seemed like a nineteen-year-old boy. And though Jeromy *was* a nineteen-year old boy, he was a tall one, six-feet-five or -six, with a surprisingly mature, solemn face topped by an unruly thatch of jet-black hair. He was a lot more imposing than any teenage sidekick had a right to be.

"Kevin?"

"That's me. C'mon in. Beer?"

"Please."

Jeromy opened the manila envelope he was carrying and pulled out a smaller envelope, a clear plastic one that held a near-mint copy of *SeaScout #14*.

"So that's it."

"Yep. You want it?"

Kevin, unexpectedly, felt like crying. He carefully opened the envelope and pulled out the comic book. The unmistakable smell of old comic book hit his nostrils, as delicately flowery as fine Chardonnay.

"Yes. I want it." *And I want you,* Kevin thought.

The guards are uncovering four large spigots in the corners of the room.

"Once your protégé has become a shipwreck, I'll be back to take care of you, Comrade SeaScout," the Red sneers. "Oh, and one thing, little Flip. You can so easily escape the fate that awaits you . . . if you'll just agree to kill SeaScout yourself."

"Never, you Commie pig! Never!"

The Red turns toward the exit.

"Ah, well. Pity. Guards, make ready."

The guards file out the door, followed by the Communist agent. The door is shut and bolted. In a moment, Flip can see the Russkie through the window, still puffing on his cigarette, his eyes evil slits.

There's the sound of valves being opened. From all four corners, water gushes into the sealed-off dungeon.

"Is a personal check okay?" Kevin had taken a close look at *#14.* If it *was* a forgery, it was the most convincing damn one imaginable.

"Of course."

Kevin pulled out his checkbook. "I've wanted this for so long. You've made me very happy, Jeromy."

For the first time that night, the tall young man smiled. It was dazzling.

Kevin handed Jeromy the check and, without asking, fetched a couple more beers. He handed one to Jeromy and sat down beside him on the couch.

"So you're nineteen, huh?" Kevin was acutely aware of how much older than the boy he was, pudgier, less attractive.

"Yeah, and let me tell you, it's not easy."

"Being nineteen?"

"Yeah. Figuring it all out, who I am, what I want." He leaned back, stretching slightly, and his leg brushed up against Kevin's and stayed there.

Kevin's cock was so hard it hurt. If he was ever going to risk a move, make his dreams real, this was the time. Kevin took his left hand and placed it, breathlessly, deliberately, on Jeromy's right thigh.

The boy stopped drinking his beer. "Hey!"

"Oh God, I'm so sorry. I'm so sorry. I'd understand if you just walked out of here and took the comic with you." Blood rushed to Kevin's face, and he felt slightly sick, then out of breath, as though he were drowning. But his hand stayed on Jeromy's thigh for a moment more, as though it were anchored there.

"Listen, it's not that I don't like you or anything. It's just that . . ."

"Jeromy, I just feel so awful about this." Like he was drowning.

The water is pouring into the room with astonishing force. Flip, tied down to the table, is surely doomed to drown.

He looks over at SeaScout, his mentor, his friend, his protector, bound naked to the wall. He can't read the expression on SeaScout's face, but the man's dick is, astonishingly, very hard, curving magnificently upward.

Flip can move his head just enough to see the water filling the room. It's a foot or two above the floor now, and rising rapidly. The end is near, and yet . . .

And yet, looking at SeaScout's gorgeous body, impassive face, eager cock, Flip feels a stirring in his crotch, too, and as the tide rises, so does the blood in his dick.

"Rick . . ." Flip begins.

"I know, Philip, I know. . . . "

"Please, let me say it. . . ."

"Philip, you don't have to say a word. . . . "

"Rick, I love you."

And the water continues its inexorable climb.

Kevin had finished telling Jeromy the story of himself, his brother, and *SeaScout #14,* though leaving out the parts about wet dreams and masturbation. Some SeaScout he'd be. He didn't feel like a superhero. He felt pathetic, felt like crying.

"Want to split another beer?" the tall, handsome boy asked.

"Sorry, that's all there was. I could maybe go out for some . . . "

Jeromy smiled again, a gentle smile. "Kevin?"

"Yeah?"

"Don't worry about it."

"But . . . "

"Kevin?"

"What?" He felt like he *was* going to break down in tears.

The boy was staring deep into his eyes, and Kevin's dick was hard, as hard as ice.

"It's just that you startled me, okay?" Jeromy smiled again, reached for Kevin's hand, and guided it back to his thigh. "Which way's your bathroom?"

Life, Kevin suddenly knew, was full of surprises.

The water is rising quickly now, almost up to SeaScout's swelling crotch, nearly reaching Flip's helpless chest.

The vicious Communist agent is watching through the window, a satisfied grin on his face, but SeaScout and Flip don't notice. They stare into eachother's eyes, and not a word need be spoken.

A sadistic, cold voice comes from a loudspeaker somewhere: "Last chance, herring boy. Kill SeaScout for me and I'll let you live."

No response.

Jeromy led Kevin, by the hand, down the hall to the bathroom.

"We could try filling the tub, but there's no way in hell both of us could fit in there."

"The shower, then?"

Jeromy reached over and turned the knobs, flipped a handle, and water started pouring from the showerhead. He stood very close to Kevin and started unbuttoning Kevin's shirt.

"Jeromy, you don't have to . . ."

"Shhh," Jeromy gently said, and he kissed Kevin on the lips. He slipped the shirt from Kevin's torso, then reached down and unbuckled the older man's belt. When he unzipped Kevin's fly, his fingers brushed against Kevin's hard dick.

"I *want* to do this," Jeromy said, and once again, Kevin felt close to tears.

And then Kevin was totally naked, and he stood in wonderment, watching as the tall, good-looking boy slowly removed his own clothing.

Jeromy's body was trim rather than muscular, was even a little bit gangly, but Kevin thought he'd never seen anything so beautiful in his entire life. The boy removed his briefs, revealing a startlingly black bush nestled between snow-white thighs. His big, thick cock was standing straight up above a generous set of balls. Kevin said a silent thank-you to God, or whoever.

They climbed clumsily into the tub, and then they were together beneath the shower, together, their flesh shiny-wet, stroking, kissing, holding each other's slippery bodies tight, cock against cock, water flowing down.

"Let me suck you off," Kevin said, silently adding *SeaScout*. But Jeromy didn't say anything. He just awkwardly got on his knees and took the older man's hard-on in his mouth.

"Oh my God," Kevin said. "Oh my God."

He could barely breathe.

And then Jeromy reached over for the bar of soap, lathered his hands up, and, taking Kevin's stiff dick all the way into his mouth, reached up and slid his soap-slick fingers up to Kevin's ass. The tight hole resisted at first but soon let one, then two fingers in. If there were tears falling from Kevin's eyes, they were invisible beneath the shower's incessant flow. Kevin didn't want to, he tried not to, but he couldn't stop himself, couldn't turn back the irresistible tide. His cock pulsed into Jeromy's mouth and the boy gulped down every salty drop.

The freezing-cold water begins to cover SeaScout's muscular thighs. Flip shivers from the spray of the onrushing flood. SeaScout flinches as the frigid liquid reaches his balls. Flip feels the water seeping beneath his back. In a matter of seconds, the rising tide engulfs the tied-down young man. A trail of bubbles escapes from his lips.

And then, just as Flip is about to breathe his last, just as SeaScout is about to watch his loyal partner die, just as SeaScout's dick is about to shoot tortured streams of cum into the flood, big red words appear across the scene: "IS THIS IT?? CAN THIS BE THE END OF SEASCOUT AND FLIP???"

After it was over, after Kevin's hand had jacked the cum from Jeromy's big dick, spurts of jizz joining the shower water spiraling down the drain, after the two men had dried off and dressed and kissed good night, promised to meet again and probably meant it, after the front door had closed and the boy was gone, Kevin found himself alone with his thoughts.

There was no way, really, to make sense of all that had happened. He'd try tomorrow, he figured, after a good night's sleep filled with underwater dreams. He walked over to the table where *SeaScout #14* lay. He just stood there looking down at the long-sought prize for a while, remembering the touch of Jeromy's lips, Jeromy's wet body against his.

Then he shook his head slightly and picked up the comic book, carefully rewrapped in its plastic shell. Beneath it, lying on the tabletop, was his $500 check, slipped there somehow by

Jeromy. Where the recipient's name was written, Jeromy had crossed off his name and written "Flip," and Kevin's own name had been replaced by "SeaScout." Across the top of the check, Jeromy had scrawled "Enjoy your comic book."

And in the lower left of the check, in the space left for comments, Jeromy, beautiful Jeromy, had written just two words: "Sail ON!"

Kevin picked up the check and looked at it a good long while. He walked over to the window, looked out at the night, the city, the lights that stood, one by one, for lives. He thought about things until he got tired of thinking, then ripped the check into little pieces. SeaScout and Flip were, after all, dead. He turned away from the window, threw the shreds of paper in the trash, picked up the plastic envelope, and pulled out *SeaScout #14.* He turned off the lights and headed for the bedroom; he figured he'd read himself to sleep. ◆

VAPORS

BY NISI SHAWL

When Tenilla turned fifteen, her mother instructed her in what she believed was the best method of masturbation. It was embarrassing, even though there was no one else around to hear her. Just Tenilla and Mom in the brown-tiled bathroom.

The tub was beige. "Lie on your back and prop your legs up on either side of the faucet before you turn it on. Leave the drain open." Mom emphasized this last point several times, as if she was worried Tenilla might forget it.

The whole idea gave her a funny feeling whenever she heard water running in the bathroom. The large, chrome-plated, hexagonal faucet, with its flared opening, took on new and uncomfortable dimensions of meaning.

Tenilla tried it. Once. She appreciated how forward-thinking her mother was, even for 1969, in acknowledging her daughter's sexual appetites. Her friends, especially the white ones, were jealous of how her mother treated her, almost like an adult. So waiting till she was alone in the apartment, Tenilla assumed the position and adjusted the water temperature. She made it a little cooler than you'd think it should be, like Mom had said.

She came right away, a quick, dull climax. Stubbornly, she stayed under the warm gush of water, trying to coax herself into another one. The water's pounding numbed her. After only a few minutes, she gave up, turned off the faucet, dried herself, and got dressed.

Her fingers were a lot more fun. She'd been practicing and hoped she could someday come with no "direct stimulation," as the marriage manual she'd stolen from the Athena Bookshop called it.

At least her mother never asked how Tenilla liked the technique she'd shared. Proving her gratitude for this, Tenilla kept the house spotless and got good grades all year. Since the divorce, Mom held two jobs and went to night school. That left hardly any time for anything else. Which was probably the real reason Mom was so liberal in her attitudes.

"I trust you to do right," she told Tenilla and her ten-year-old sister, Bee, taking their suitcases out of the Mercury's trunk. "I've raised you the best I can. The rest is up to you." The two girls were being sent by Greyhound to Aunt Cherry's in Paw Paw; Bee for the whole summer, Tenilla for six weeks.

Aunt Cherry's pace was much slower than Mom's. She was retired, not exactly an aunt, and old. She kept a garden. There was a little weeding, but Aunt Cherry laid thick straw wherever she didn't want stuff to grow.

"You can do anything you put your mind to," she told Tenilla. "And you can do it two ways. Ain't neither of 'em wrong, but one's hard, and one's right."

The house was smaller than the apartment she was used to, but Tenilla had much more privacy. There was one bedroom, instead of two, and of course Aunt Cherry had that. But while Bee slept on the little gray couch in the living room, under a dark green cover printed with white lilies, Tenilla took the cot on the screened-in porch. It was cool out there, so she had a quilt over her, soft squares of pink and blue and brown. She spent the short nights alone. She loved how the porch smelled when the rain fell hissing all around her. Not one drop touched her, though the air was drenched.

When the rain stopped, the water remained. The sun struck through clouds, raising swirls of steam, morning fogs and evening mists that clung to Tenilla's calves as she crossed Aunt Cherry's overgrown lawn.

She spent the long days by the lake, watching the clouds melt into the water, the water lift itself into the sky.

She was in the bottom of a bowl, a boiling pot. Each day the blue sky on top collected condensation from the lake below. Tenilla sent her breath up with the moist exhalations of the plants and the other animals living along the lake's edge. It came back down to her faithfully, laden with lessons. She absorbed them with the atmosphere, applied them when the lights went out.

One night, despite the coolness, Tenilla tossed off the quilt. Her hands drifted over her skin in the dark, their hovering warmth stirring tiny hairs. She let her fingertips fall softly, barely pattering, exploring outward along each arm, sweeping down her breasts to her sides, following her belly's curve. The sound of the rain found her, filled her as she eased her thighs apart. It steadied, settled in. Holding her outer lips open, Tenilla touched everything between them with the same gentle insistence. And she came. Again. Came. Again. Short bursts blended into longer rhythms, fading away as the sky paled.

That was the best time, but there were others almost as good.

Then the six weeks were up.

It was time for her to go home. Tenilla took the Greyhound by herself this time. The driver came back to her seat and shut the window. A smell like stale ice cubes blew up from the vent beneath it.

The town felt empty. Her friends were busy, or away. They'd gotten used to her being gone. The boy she'd been half-interested in was with someone else.

Tenilla looked up a lot. Buildings blocked the clouds, kept her from seeing how they formed and fell to pieces. She had the bedroom to herself but missed the porch, the melting air, and made little progress.

The marriage manual no longer inspired her. Nothing did. Her hands felt numb, her fingers harsh and clumsy. She could barely come.

One morning, as she fixed her mom's instant coffee, she saw a tiny puff of steam above the kettle's spout. The silver droplets vanished speedily in the dark, dry atmosphere of the apartment. Not before Tenilla noticed they were there, though.

The clerks at the Athena were kind and helpful. That made Tenilla feel bad. She *bought* these books. June Rice's *Herbal*. Parvati's *Personal Care Compendium*. She wanted others, but these two took a big bite out of the allowance money she'd saved, and she'd need some for supplies.

She had no idea what she was doing. She tried to remember what Aunt Cherry grew in her garden. Roses. Those were recommended. Marigolds. Parvati called them calendula. And at the lake's edge there'd been horsetails, which was *equisetum* in Latin, and *mentha,* mint. June Rice suggested finding these things at the drugstore, but all she could come up with at Van Avery's was mint candy, chocolate-coated cream patties. She bought them so no one would think she was stealing.

The hippie food co-op up near campus had everything, even the horsetails.

She heated water in the spaghetti pot, measured in her herbs, and, draping a white towel over her head, leaned in to inhale.

No. Not the same. Not enough.

She should have stayed there, at the lake. Would she ever feel that way again?

She cried in bed and fell asleep with a wet face.

She woke up in a more optimistic mood. You could do anything you put your mind to. Aunt Cherry had said so. Staying at the lake would have been a lot less work, but she could still do it, she could still bring herself back to where she'd been. She could do it the hard way. Only it wouldn't be easy.

This was one of Mom's long days, and she'd gone out already. Four hours on the switchboard at the unemployment office, five more at the phone company, and an evening class at Western. There was plenty of time to plan and prepare.

Tenilla damp-mopped the kitchen floor, though it was clean. She wiped down the windows, leaving them dotted with moisture. The morning sun sparkled in each crystalline bead. They thickened and ran in streams when the four pots on the stovetop started to simmer. The rag rug rolled up against the door to the dining room, red and sodden, kept out the slightest coolness. The sink was filling. She turned the tap to a trickle, took off her pajamas, and opened the oven.

The shiny roaster gleamed with sweat, dense clouds rising from the edges of its domed lid. She set it carefully on the floor in the center of a white towel, which was, like everything else at this point, damp.

She removed the lid. The unmeasured remnant of her herbs stewed in the water. Their potency thickened the air visibly, making each breath three times sweeter than the one before.

Perspiration dripped from Tenilla's eyebrows, from her broad nose, salting the steam. She stood, straddling the pan, and the tendrils rose along her legs, drawn up by the sun.

She shone. She was golden. She parted the rays of her heat-soaked pubic hair. Drops formed on her inner lips, loading themselves with her scent. Inhaling, Tenilla slumped forward, then arched to expand her lungs. The coiling vapor insinuated itself along ten thousand pathways, filling Tenilla's tree-like alveoli with its wetness. It invaded her blood. Her pulse doubled. Her heart drove all excess downward, further engorging the sensitive folds of flesh, exposing new surfaces. Her swelling clitoris spangled itself with condensation. She felt the birth of each brilliant globule, its growth, its liquid coalescence. Every single one was a world, swimming with sensations, dazzlingly distinct. Their edges shimmered. Then the waters came together.

She was on her elbows, on her knees. Sobbing. Tears ran from her eyes, saliva from her mouth. Her back racked with convulsions, flexed hips and head together and apart, in and out, up and down. Spray flew from her in arcs, spattering the floor.

Gradually, her spasms grew gentler. They subsided, and she sank to the ground. Beside her, the roasting pan still radiated a comforting warmth. She curled around it, resting.

The light from the windows shifted till it was indirect. The kitchen dimmed and cooled. Tenilla stretched, sat up, stretched again. In a high corner a slow, vague stirring showed where the last of the steam cloud lingered. Tenilla watched it without seeing it, thinking of the future.

Two more weeks of summer vacation. Then the equinox, and its storms. Then snow. Then the thaws of spring. The waters of the world were her teachers. She knew now she would listen to them, and learn from them, and love them all. All of them, in their turn. ♦

HOW IT STARTED

BY MARY ANNE MOHANRAJ

When a hot new dyke moves to Berkeley, you've got only a tiny window of time in which to make your move. If you don't move quick, she'll be snapped up by someone else, and you'll be left alone in your bed—wet fingers for company, waxing the saddle and wishing for love.

It was late at the Calyx, past midnight, and the floor was packed with couples, hip to hip, breast to breast. But she was dancing alone, shimmying to the beat with a circle of space around her, head thrown back and sweat dripping off her body. She was so fine—skin like toasted coconut, lips dark and lush. A tight white tank over huge breasts; God, each one looked bigger than my head. Curving belly. Hips that moved in deep, wide circles, like she was fucking the air. No one I'd seen before. I didn't know why no one was making a move on her, but I wasn't going to wait to find out.

I let my body move to the music, let it carry me over to her.

We were dancing alone, a foot or so apart, and then a little closer, a little closer still. That's when her eyes opened—dark green. Yum—I've got a thing for green eyes. She smiled at me, slow and lazy, and I slid closer, just an inch or two away from those glorious breasts. Dancing hard, sweat flicking off me as I shook my ass, arms up in the air, arching my back and hoping my breasts looked bigger than they were. Our sweat mingling in the air, falling to the floor, the whole place hot and damp with horny cunts writhing to the music. She opened her mouth a little then, and I almost just went for it, almost dove in for the kind of hot wet kiss that could convince a girl that she wanted to go home with *me* tonight, that I could show her the best time she'd ever seen. And that's when she said it.

"I have a girlfriend. She just doesn't dance. Sorry."

Fuck. I kept dancing; there wasn't much else to do.

"I'm Janna," she said.

"Susan. You been in town long?" I knew the answer to that one, but I had to try, had to keep the conversation going. I was still hoping it wasn't serious, that I had a chance. Not that I was the sort of girl who tried to break up relationships . . . but if a couple was already on the rocks and you just came along at the right time, that wasn't really your fault. You might even be doing them a favor.

"Just moved out. I'm teaching at the U." She paused there; I hoped that she was going to say something about having just met her girlfriend, or say that it wasn't working out, or that the woman was mean or just plain nuts. Instead, she said, "Carla came with me. We've been together eight years."

Goddamn it. That was it, then.

She disappeared into the crowd after the song ended; I figured she was out of my life. But in the next few weeks I kept running into her. At the co-op, buying groceries, we'd be picking out cucumbers and carrots side by side. At the bookstore—not one of the regular bookstores, but the SF one—we reached for the same copy of Delany's latest. Across the counter at Sushi-A-Float, I watched her slide sea urchin into her mouth, watched it move down her throat. By the third encounter, I was dying of unsatisfied lust. The worst time was Saturday night at the hot tubs; she left just as I was walking in—we stopped and exchanged a few words. And even though I was with a cute redhead, a girl with sweet, thick nipples and a fat ass just right for grabbing, I fantasized about Janna the whole time I was fucking the girl in the tub. I had three fingers in the redhead's pussy and my mouth on her nipple; I was dizzy with the heat, and every curl of steam rising from the water reminded me of the black curls of Janna's hair, made me wonder if it was just as curly down below.

I got the redhead off, but only just, and she never spoke to me again. Guess she could tell my mind wasn't really on her. That was when I lost it. I'd never tried to break a couple up before, and I wasn't going to try now, not really. I didn't need to date Janna—I just had to have her, had to fuck her. Just once.

I signed up for one of her classes at the U. She was teaching some feminist theory crap; I had never gone for that stuff, but I read up on it, just in case she called on me. Not that I talked much in class. It was summer term, as hot as Berkeley ever got—seventies or eighties most days, cool crisp mornings followed by brief heat. I wore the skimpiest clothes I had, and when I ran out of those, I raided the used-clothing stores, looking for more. Pale mesh tops with dark push-up bras; short tight skirts and tall black boots; thin white T-shirts with no bra at all; cutoffs and ankle bracelets and bare feet with the toenails done in red . . . every sexy look I could think of. I sat in the front of the class for weeks and alternated crossing and uncrossing and recrossing my legs. No panties, red silk bikinis, black lace thongs, damp white cotton. I leaned forward in my chair, rested my elbows and breasts on the table. I didn't try to catch her eye; that would have made it just that little bit too obvious. She would have had to confront the fact that I was deliberately fucking with the teacher, and that the teacher was enjoying it. Janna *was* enjoying it. I could tell. I watched out of the corner of my eye, in quick glances. Her face got flushed when I uncrossed my legs; she called on the others, but she kept looking at me.

The day it climbed up to ninety, I had a Coke with ice in front of me. I kept fishing ice cubes out of the cup, sucking them slowly until they were half gone, then chewing the rest. I wondered if she had heard what I had heard—that girls who chewed ice were sexually frustrated. God knew it was true. Janna was wearing a thin white dress that day—opaque, but thin enough that it clung to her curving body, moving as she moved, damp with her sweat. Little trickles of sweat slid from behind her ears, down her neck and collarbone, into the V of her dress, disappearing between those breasts. I was so thirsty, and hot enough that I couldn't think straight. So I pushed it further than I ever had before—I fished out another ice cube and used it to trace the same path on my own body, right there in class. Anyone could have seen me. Started behind an ear, down my neck, across the collarbone, shivering with pleasure. I was carefully looking at the chalkboard, but I could feel her eyes on me—and then I dropped the ice down the front of my shirt. It slid down between my breasts, coming to rest for a moment in my belly button. It was fucking cold—too cold to leave it there. So I shimmied a little and it slid down farther, coming to rest where my thighs met, melting against my clit, creating a little wet puddle on the wooden seat underneath me. Janna watched everything.

When the class ended, she waited until the other students had filed out. I sat in my chair, looking at nothing, hot and wet and a little scared. She had a right to be mad. She walked up to me, stopped in front of my desk.

"Drop the class," she said. "You're distracting my students."

I nodded.

Then she reached out and picked up another piece of ice. She placed it on my shirt and held it there, just above the nipple. Let it melt a second, dripping Coke-sticky cold water down onto my nipple, which popped straight up. She watched me, watched my breath catch, watched me swallow. Then she dropped the ice back in the cup, smiled sweetly, and spoke again.

"Just one rule. Carla gets to watch."

Oh shit.

I'd done some group stuff in college; everyone did, right? When dyke club meetings got late, when everyone got drunk and giddy. You ended up sprawled over some girl's couch, feeling up someone's breasts by candlelight while someone else felt up yours. But none of those had ever gone all that far; clothes had mostly stayed on—they just got pushed out of the way. All the real screwing I'd done had been one-on-one. Still, it didn't sound like Carla would be doing anything—just watching. Watching would be okay, right? I could just ignore her, and it would be worth it—it would *so* be worth it to get my hands on Janna's breasts, on her belly and hips and ass. I wanted to grind my pubic bone against her clit; I wanted my fingers fucking her, in and out, fast and hard and sweet. I wanted her screaming, and I wanted it bad. So I said yes.

We walked back to their house, not touching, a foot of space between us, my body humming with desire.

Carla worked at home; she was there when we walked in, leaning over a computer, long brown hair falling in front of her face. She turned around when we walked in the door, and I could tell right away that she knew; she knew exactly why we were there, in the middle of the afternoon, when Janna should have been holding office hours. Carla looked at us and knew. I was ready for her to get mad, to get weepy, but instead she smiled. It was a wicked grin, stretching her mouth wide and showing teeth. That grin took her plain pale face—a face I wouldn't have looked at twice in a club—and turned it into something else again. Something maybe a little dangerous.

Janna said, "This is Susan. She wants to play."

"You two go ahead and get started. I'll be there in a minute." And she turned back to the computer and started typing again.

Shit. I couldn't believe she was so fucking casual about the whole thing. Did Janna bring women home like this all the time?

What was going on with these two anyway? But then Janna was taking my hand, leading me through the house to the bedroom, pulling me onto the bed, and I didn't give a damn anymore. So Carla didn't mind if Janna fucked other women—this was my problem? Hell, no. Janna's mouth was on mine, moving hot and wet, and her fingers were unbuttoning my cutoffs, pulling them off; I lifted my ass to help, and in a couple of minutes I was naked and she was too, and we were writhing together like two fish on a wet dock—fuck Carla!

I finally got my mouth on Janna's breast—just as gorgeous naked as I'd hoped it would be, and even bigger than I'd thought—and sucked hard, pressing my face against it, smothering myself eagerly in all that soft flesh. I couldn't breathe, and didn't want to; she was on top of me, her body crushing me into the bed. I liked it; I wanted more. I tried to reach down to her cunt, but her hands grabbed my wrists and pulled them up over my head, pinning me down. Her thigh pushed my legs apart and pressed against my crotch; then her hip was grinding into me, shoving me down hard against the mattress. She was pushing me, pushing me up and over, and I was moaning. Usually it was me making the other girl come, *me* making *her* scream, but Janna had me down and begging for it, and when she bit my nipple I came hard. I came once, then again, and it was when I was gearing up to come for a third time that I noticed that somewhere in there, my wrists had gotten tied to a bedpost. Fuck.

I tugged against the rope—tight. Opened my eyes, and there was Carla, comfortable in a rocking chair, snuggled up in an afghan, of all the weird-ass things—a fucking orange afghan.

She was wearing granny glasses, and if she'd been a couple of decades older, she could have *been* someone's granny. But I knew that *she* was the one who had tied me up while Janna was busy distracting me, and she was definitely the one grinning now, watching us. And when Janna paused for breath, Carla was the one who reached out to the bedside table, who picked up a giant economy-size tube of Wet lube, and who said, "I think she could use a good fisting, honey," as she handed it to Janna. Then she sat back in the chair and started it rocking, her eyes fixed on mine.

I could have said something. But instead, I closed my eyes. I bit my lip and lay back; I wrapped my hands around the ropes and let Janna drizzle lube into my snatch. A little to start—then she was swirling her fingers around the mouth of it, getting every millimeter of skin wet. It had been pretty wet already, but for a fisting it was going to need to be a lot wetter. Or so I'd heard.

She rubbed my clit until I started squirming on the sheets again. Then she slid a finger into my hole. Two. Three. No problem. Four was easy. I had taken four plenty of times. And when she slid her thumb in there, I spread my thighs wider, inviting her in. That part I knew how to do. She fucked me silently—she hadn't said a word this entire time, had hardly spoken since we'd left her class. But I could hear her breathing, could feel one of her hands pressing down on my open thigh and the other sliding into me, in and out. More lube. She was doing something with her hand—spiraling it as she slid in and out of me. Pushing a little harder each time, pushing closer to the knuckles. I wanted her to go fast, to get it over with—to just push past the pain, like the first time I got fucked with a strap-on. But Janna went slower and slower. And she was quiet enough that I could hear Carla start to whisper.

"Come on, Susie. You can do it. Relax—you gotta relax and let her into you. Open up wide and let her into your wet cunt, your sopping pussy. You want her to—you want her so bad. . . ."

Janna was pouring more lube onto me now, cold at first, thick and wet, coating my thighs and cunt and the sheets and her hand, fucking in and out of me.

"I saw it at the club; I watched you make up to my girl, and I knew you were dying for her, you wanted her so bad. So give it up, baby. Relax and let it go, let her have you, let her take you."

She was pushing harder, pushing hard enough that it hurt, just a little. Pushing down, and her fingers pressing against that spot that felt so good but made me feel like I was gonna pee. And I was twisting under her hand, or trying to—I couldn't help it—but she kept my hips pinned down with one hand and fucked me with the other. In and out.

"We want you to let us fuck you, baby, and it's the least you can do, little tease, little slut. You pretend you're a top, but what you really want is for someone to take you and fuck you hard, push you up and over the edge—"

I was moaning now, pulling hard on the ropes and glad they were there, moaning loud enough that I almost couldn't hear her anymore. I was so close, so fucking close.

" . . . and you want it bad enough that you're willing to beg for it from someone you know you aren't supposed to touch. So come on, baby girl . . . come on. . . ."

And that was it, Janna's hand slid into me with a quiet pop, a sucking noise, and it didn't hurt at all. It was in me. Then she started moving it. Moving inside me, her whole fucking hand. She opened it up and closed it, her fingers reaching up and into me, like she wasn't just fucking my cunt, like she was fucking *all* of me, and I was shivering and screaming before long, coming up and over and over again.

It went on for a long time.

When they were done with me, Carla untied me, still grinning. Janna and I showered, giggling off and on. I was pretty high on an endorphin rush; my thighs were trembling and my head was spinning. Dropping the soap was funny, and almost slipping on it was hilarious. I didn't know why Janna was giggling too, but I didn't care. I was just glad she'd enjoyed herself. Janna soaped my back and I did hers; we washed each other's pussies clean. That was all good.

By the time we started drying off, I was coming down from my high, the giggles disappearing and exhaustion taking over. I started wondering if this was it, if they were done with me. Maybe they picked up a different girl every week—it was possible. That should have been fine with me—all I'd wanted was to fuck Janna, right? And even if she'd fucked me instead, or they both had, I couldn't complain that I was unsatisfied. There was no reason for me to feel blue—but I did.

My mood got worse as I got dressed—Janna disappeared to go find Carla. When I joined them in their sunny yellow kitchen, they were sharing a glass of water. They looked so fucking cute; Janna leaning against Carla, the glass cradled in her hands. I shoved my hands in my pockets so they couldn't see them shake; I was ready to storm off, pissed for no reason I could explain.

Then Carla said, "Hey, that was great! Do you need to take off, or do you want to stick around and talk, maybe have dinner?"

Dinner. I wasn't sure what came with dinner—maybe something complicated—maybe more than I wanted in the end. It had been a pretty strange day. But for now . . .

"Dinner sounds good."

I took my hands out of my pockets as Janna handed me the glass, and drank deep. ♦

ABOUT THE CONTRIBUTORS

• JEFFREY S. CHAPMAN is a doctoral candidate at the University of Utah, in Salt Lake City. He received a M.F.A. degree in fiction from Sarah Lawrence College.

• MARY GAITSKILL is the author of the story collections *Bad Behavior* and *Because They Wanted To*, as well as the novel *Two Girls, Fat and Thin*. Her stories and essays have appeared in many publications, including *The New Yorker, Harper's, Esquire, Tin House, Salon.com,* and *The Village Voice*.

• J. HARTMAN is a writer, editor, and native Californian who has written software documentation, fiction, and reviews. *Clean Sheets* has published some of the fiction and reviews.

• Librarian by day and pornographer by night, CHRIS JONES lives with longtime partner, Tim, in upstate New York. Chris's work has appeared in *Blue Food* and *Wired Hard 3*.

• DIANE KEPLER merely raises an eyebrow when people ask whether her story ideas are culled from real life. She contributed fiction and nonfiction to the premiere issue of *Clean Sheets,* and further concupiscent tales appear in *Aqua Erotica* and *Best Bisexual Erotica 2*.

• LOREN MACLEOD is the penname of a magazine editor who works for the Smithsonian Institution in Washington, D.C.

She has been writing short fiction since 1996. "Giselle" was inspired by a particularly vivid dream.

• JACK MURNIGHAN has a B.A. in philosophy and semiotics and a Ph.D. in medieval literature. He writes a weekly column on the history of sexy literature, "Jack's Naughty Bits," for *Nerve.com* (where he served as editor in chief). A collection of these columns, entitled *The Naughty Bits*, was published in June 2001. He coedited the anthology *Full Frontal Fiction* and has had short stories chosen for *The Best American Erotica* anthologies of 1999, 2000, and 2001.

• BILL NOBLE (noblebill@aol.com) is a widely published writer living in Northern California. He has received the National Looking Glass Award for poetry and been recognized for fiction by the Southwest Writers Conference. He is an editor of the online magazine of literary erotica, *Clean Sheets*.

• NISI SHAWL's fiction has appeared in *Dark Matter: A Century of Speculative Fiction from the African Diaspora* and in *Isaac Asimov's SF Magazine*. She writes features and articles for the Seattle alternative weekly, *The Stranger*.

• SIMON SHEPPARD is the author of *Hotter Than Hell and Other Stories*, and the coeditor of *Rough Stuff: Tales of Gay Men, Sex, and Power*. His work has been widely anthologized in books including *The Best American Erotica* and *Best Gay Erotica*. He can be found online at www.simonsheppard.com.

• A winner of the Henry Miller Award in 1992, DAVE SMEDS has written over sixty erotic short stories for such magazines as *Penthouse Letters*, *Club International*, and *Mayfair*, and for anthologies such as *Sirens*, *FleshFantastic*, and *TechnoSex*. Circlet

Press collected eleven of these tales and published them under the byline Reed Manning as *Earthly Pleasures*, a volume praised for its "playfulness, sense of wonder, and crispness of tone."

• CECILIA TAN is the author of *Black Feathers*, *The Velderet*, and *Telepaths Don't Need Safewords*. Her erotic short stories have appeared in dozens of venues, including *Best American Erotica*, *Ms.*, *Nerve.com*, and *Aqua Erotica*. Biographical details can be found at www.ceciliatan.com.

• CONNIE WILKINS exercises her libidinous imagination in western Massachusetts and the mountains of New Hampshire. Under the name Sacchi Green, her stories have appeared in *Best Lesbian Erotica 1999* through *2002*, *Best Women's Erotica 2001* and *2002*, *Best Transgender Erotica*, and an assortment of themed anthologies, including *Zaftig*, *Set in Stone*, and *Shameless*.

FOR KARINA

Acknowledgments

I must gratefully praise my stellar staff at *Strange Horizons,* who kept the magazine running smoothly despite an editor in chief on the road all summer, engrossed in anthology-editing. I'd also like to thank those friends who kindly put me up as I traveled from Salt Lake City to Chicago to the Bay Area to Portland to Seattle to Los Angeles to Salt Lake again— Kevin Whyte, J. Hartman, David Horwich, Kirsten Brumley, and Lisette Bross. You were lovely hosts.

—MARY ANNE MOHANRAJ

Special thanks to Rachel Kahan, Jessica Marshall, John Meils, and Megan Worman.

—MELCHER MEDIA

About the Editor

Mary Anne Mohanraj (www.mamohanraj.com) is the author of *Torn Shapes of Desire,* editor of *Aqua Erotica*, and consulting editor for *Herotica 7.* She has been published in many anthologies and magazines, including *Herotica 6, Best American Erotica 1999,* and *Best Women's Erotica 2000* and *2001.* Mohanraj founded the erotic webzine, *Clean Sheets* (www.clean-sheets.com) and serves as editor-in-chief for the speculative fiction webzine *Strange Horizons* (www.strangehorizons.com).

Mohanraj also moderates the EROS Workshop and is a 1997 graduate of Clarion West. She has received degrees in Writing and English from Mills College and the University of Chicago, and is currently a doctoral student in Fiction and Literature at the University of Utah. She received the Scowcroft Award for fiction in Spring 2001.

About Melcher Media

Melcher Media is an award-winning content producer and book packager based in New York City.

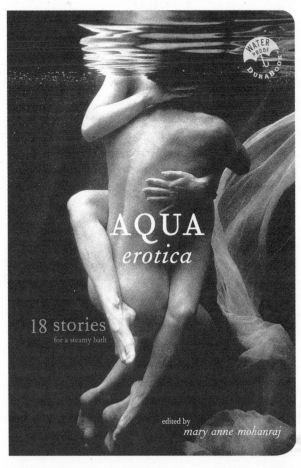

AQUA
erotica

18 stories
for a steamy bath

edited by
mary anne mohanraj

"Hot, wet, and extremely well-crafted." —*Kirkus Reviews*